WILLING
TO WED THE
RANCHER

Books by Jody Hedlund

High Country Ranch
Waiting for the Rancher
Willing to Wed the Rancher
A Wife for the Rancher
Wrangling the Wandering Rancher
Wishing for the Rancher's Love

Colorado Cowgirls
Committing to the Cowgirl
Cherishing the Cowgirl
Convincing the Cowgirl
Captivated by the Cowgirl
Claiming the Cowgirl: A Novella

Colorado Cowboys
A Cowboy for Keeps
The Heart of a Cowboy
To Tame a Cowboy
Falling for the Cowgirl
The Last Chance Cowboy

A Shanahan Match
Calling on the Matchmaker

Bride Ships: New Voyages
Finally His Bride
His Treasured Bride

Bride Ships Series
A Reluctant Bride

The Runaway Bride
A Bride of Convenience
Almost a Bride

Orphan Train Series
An Awakened Heart: A Novella
With You Always
Together Forever
Searching for You

Beacons of Hope Series
Out of the Storm: A Novella
Love Unexpected
Hearts Made Whole
Undaunted Hope
Forever Safe
Never Forget

Hearts of Faith Collection
The Preacher's Bride
The Doctor's Lady
Rebellious Heart

Michigan Brides Collection
Unending Devotion
A Noble Groom
Captured by Love

Historical
Luther and Katharina
Newton & Polly

HIGH COUNTRY RANCH SERIES

WILLING
TO WED THE
RANCHER

JODY HEDLUND

NORTHERN LIGHTS PRESS

Willing to Wed the Rancher

Northern Lights Press

© 2024 by Jody Hedlund

Jody Hedlund Print Edition

ISBN: 979-8-9896277-1-4

Jody Hedlund www.jodyhedlund.com

Cover Design by Hannah Linder

Cover images from Shutterstock

1

SUMMIT COUNTY, COLORADO
MAY 1879

Drats. Mr. Meyer was going to propose to her today.

Clarabelle Oakley pressed a hand to her racing heart as she peeked out the parlor window and watched Eric Meyer open the front wrought-iron gate.

Not only was he wearing his best suit with his face scrubbed and beard trimmed, but determination was written in every line of his expression as he closed the gate and started up the flagstone path.

She let the lacy curtain fall back into place. For heaven's sake. What should she do?

Her muscles tightened with the need to flee, and she spun to face the dozen or so children milling about the room. Her gaze darted past them to the side parlor door that led to the breakfast room and the kitchen. From there she could slip out the back door of the house and hide until he was gone.

Or she could hide under the desk. It was situated against the far wall, past the benches that filled the center of their makeshift school. She'd knock the tin of pencils to the floor, then duck down behind the desk and pick them up until Eric collected Bianca and Dieter and left.

Yes, that would work.

She took a step toward the desk, but a tug on her skirt halted her.

Bianca stood in front of her, peering up with wide blue eyes. "Miss Oakley, my shoe is unlaced again." At five years of age, the little girl was a waif, only reaching Clarabelle's waist. With dainty features and silky dark hair, Bianca was as pretty as an angel. If only her behavior were just as angelic.

But the child, like her brother Dieter, was more than a handful and in much need of a woman's—a mother's—guidance. And if Eric Meyer had his way, he intended to make Clarabelle the mother of his two children.

As the door opened in the front hallway, a fresh burst of panic shot through Clarabelle. She wasn't opposed to becoming a mother to Bianca and Dieter. That wasn't the issue. She'd grown to love the pair over the past year of helping in the schoolroom as the teacher's assistant.

The problem was that she didn't love Eric. He was such a nice man—earnest, hardworking, and even a little handsome, but she didn't feel a spark of interest in him, not even the slightest flicker.

She couldn't—wouldn't—wed a man she didn't absolutely adore with all her heart. She was simply too much of a romantic to marry out of convenience rather than for love.

Maybe if she mussed her hair or made herself unappealing, she could dissuade Eric. She tugged at her coil of hair and pulled some of the strands loose. Then she untucked part of her simple blue brocade blouse from her matching skirt. Finally, she rubbed the chalk dust covering her hands onto her cheek.

A peek into the mirror above the mantel showed her to be slightly frazzled, looking more like her twin sister Clementine, who was always less put together. Though they were identical, with willowy bodies, slender faces, wide green eyes, and blond-red hair, Clarabelle had fairer skin, mostly because Clementine refused to wear her bonnet outside half the time.

Clarabelle tugged another strand of hair loose, then sighed. Messy hair wouldn't distract Eric from his mission. No, she needed to hide.

She side-stepped Bianca, but the girl clung to Clarabelle's skirt like a vine to a trellis. "Would you show me again how to make the bunny ears?"

As much as Clarabelle wanted to pry the child loose and race out of the room, she forced herself to respond calmly. "How do you ask politely, Bianca?"

"Please?" The little girl's eyes were expectant.

How could anyone refuse such a look? Especially knowing the child didn't have a mother at home to care about her or train her or shower her with love.

Of course, Eric was a good father. There was no doubt about that. Since emigrating from Germany six years ago, the Meyers had been one of the Oakleys' neighbors, and though they'd kept mostly to themselves, they'd always been friendly. Clarabelle wasn't sure what had lured Eric and his wife Luisa to Colorado initially, but they'd come to the fertile Blue River valley, settled on a small spread, and started farming the land.

Dieter had been a newborn when everyone had rallied to help the Meyers build a log cabin and barn that summer. Clarabelle had only been a girl of thirteen at the time, and at twenty-four, Eric had seemed so old.

Now that she was nineteen, his thirty years didn't seem quite so distant. Even so, she had a hard time thinking of him as an eligible suitor, especially when the memories of him with Luisa, particularly from those early days when the two had been obviously in love with each other, were so vivid.

Clarabelle felt sorry for Eric. She really did. He'd lost the woman he loved and his youngest child during an outbreak of scarlet fever last year. He'd almost lost Bianca, too, but Clarabelle's ma, who had worked tirelessly to help the family, had managed to save the child.

Before Clarabelle could wrestle herself free from Bianca's hold on her skirt, Eric's broad frame filled the parlor doorway. He scanned the room, his gaze coming to land upon her forcefully enough to knock the air from her lungs.

The determination on his face was even more intense now that he was inside. Yes, he was most definitely planning to propose today. She wouldn't have been surprised if he'd called out to her above the hubbub of the children and asked for her hand in front of everyone.

Mrs. Grover, who was talking with several of the older children near the door, paused and stared at Eric, as though she, too, recognized that something was different about him today.

With her graying hair, the matron was old enough and wealthy enough to spend her days in leisure. But after moving to Breckenridge two years ago with her husband, who was an assayer of gold and silver, she spent her days leading one charitable organization after another, working tirelessly to improve the small town. Just last year she'd petitioned to have a school built, but with only a small number of families having young children, the petition had been delayed.

Instead of putting aside her plans for the school, Mrs. Grover had started teaching in her parlor. Since she knew about Clarabelle's aspiration to become a teacher, she'd asked Clarabelle to assist in the classroom, and Clarabelle had eagerly done so until Ma had taken to her bed after Pa's death.

For the past four months, Clarabelle hadn't been able to assist in the school every day because she'd been tending Ma much of the time. After Ma's passing two weeks ago, Clarabelle hadn't missed a day of school since the funeral. Being away from the ranch and spending time with the children helped to keep her mind off missing Ma.

"Miss Oakley?" Eric's voice squeaked, and he cleared his throat loudly.

At the sight of her father, Bianca let go of Clarabelle's skirt and skipped toward Eric, a smile lighting up her little face. "Father!"

Dieter, in the middle of bargaining with several other boys, pocketed something and then straightened, his eyes now on his father. The six-year-old had the same fair hair, blue eyes, and stocky build as Eric—was a miniature version except without the facial hair.

As Bianca reached her father, she threw her arms around his legs and clung to him.

Eric absently patted her head but was still looking at Clarabelle. "Miss Oakley? Would you do me the honor of—of—"

Clarabelle's heart ceased beating. It was already difficult enough for her to say no to anyone privately. It would be nearly impossible if he proposed to her in front of Mrs. Grover and all the children.

She waved a hand toward the spacious hallway with its ivy-print wallpaper and matching ivy-print rugs. "Let's speak alone, shall we, Mr. Meyer?"

He opened his mouth as if to protest or propose, but then he closed it and nodded.

Clarabelle rapidly crossed the room, and thankfully, Eric backed out of the doorway.

A few minutes later, she stood on the front wraparound porch with him while Bianca and Dieter waited in his wagon, parked in front of the home. With its gabled roof, rising turret, and decorative woodwork around the windows, the home was just as lovely on the outside as it was inside.

Eric had doffed his hat and now twisted the brim, just like he had that day of Ma's funeral when he'd first made his intentions known. They'd been standing at the graveside with many others, and Eric had approached her to offer his condolences. Bianca had been the one to bring up Eric proposing marriage: *"Father says you can become our new Mutti now that you're not needed at your home."*

Eric had been embarrassed by Bianca's bold statement, but he hadn't denied it. Instead, he'd asked Clarabelle to think about it and said he'd pay her a visit soon.

She'd tried to hint that she wasn't the right woman for him and that she wasn't ready for marriage or a family, but obviously she hadn't hinted strongly enough. Now, today, she was left with no choice but to set him straight.

"Miss Oakley." He stared down the gravel street lined with large Victorian-style homes just as elegant and elaborate as the Grovers'. With the recent discovery of silver in the hills around Summit County and the influx of settlers, most of the homes were new, having been constructed over the past year or two.

As more of the school children stepped outside onto the front porch, Eric paused again, waiting for them to pass.

She had to speak first, before he did, so as soon as the children were out of hearing range, she forced the words out that needed to be said. "Please don't, Mr. Meyer."

He'd opened his mouth to say something but now stalled and studied her face, as if trying to read what she'd left unspoken.

"I'm too young." She tried to offer him the least hurtful explanation without having to tell him that she couldn't see herself with him—not now, not ever.

"You will be a goot Mutter to Bianca and Dieter." His statement was filled with a quiet desperation she didn't understand.

"You'll find a different woman—"

"Nein." A frown wrinkled his brow. "Time is run out."

"Time is run out for what?"

He glanced both ways up and down the street, and his narrowed eyes seemed to take in every detail as though he were expecting enemies to jump out from behind buildings. Then he leaned in and lowered his voice. "I fear for mine safety, Miss Oakley."

She followed his gaze, half expecting to see men hunkered down ready to shoot at them. But from what she could tell, the only people present were several children walking away from the Grovers', and one of the mothers of a young student, hurrying up the cross street toward the school.

"I have no one for them left." Eric reached out as though he intended to take her hands.

She shifted her hands behind her back and clasped them together tightly.

He crossed his arms instead. "Only mine Bruder. He is in Deutschland and will not answer mine letters."

"What about Luisa's family?"

"They do not write back either."

She couldn't fathom being cut off from family, not with how close she'd always been to her own. What had happened to create such a rift? It wasn't her place to ask. But she could offer him reassurance that she'd help him just like her ma had done. It was the neighborly way. "If anything happens to you, I'll gladly help you and the children."

"As mine wife?"

She had to tell him no. She had to. But even as she tried to force the word from her mouth, something else came out instead. "I can't promise that. At least, not now." Maybe someday she might feel differently about him. That was possible, wasn't it?

He was watching Bianca and Dieter on the wagon bench as they started to squabble with each other. "I will take goot care of you, give you everything I own."

"That's not necessary—"

"You will use it to care for Dieter and Bianca." Eric's gaze shifted back to her, pinning her with his intensity.

This conversation wasn't going the way she wanted. If she weren't careful, she'd find herself wed to him before the week was finished.

If only she had some of Clementine's pluck, but her twin sister had gotten all the boldness for the both of them, and then some.

"Please?" Eric's tone dropped to a hoarse whisper.

How could she refuse him? She couldn't. That was the truth. "Okay."

He expelled a breath. "Goot."

What had she just agreed to? Certainly not to marriage. She'd simply offered to help with his children if anything happened to him.

He cocked his head toward his wagon. "I will give you a ride home, yes?"

"Thank you, but I have my horse." The ride to High Country Ranch, known by most as High C Ranch, was only a couple of miles north of town, and she liked the time to think and be alone after the busy day with the children.

Placing his hat back on his head, he nodded and took the first step before halting. He hesitated a moment before facing her again, his eyes somber, his expression serious. "Then we will marry in one week?"

Her hands began to tremble, and she clutched them together tightly. Apparently he thought she was willing to wed him. How could she set him straight? "I think you misunderstood me, Mr. Meyer."

"You do not want to rush."

"Right." That was sort of what she'd alluded to.

"Then two weeks?"

She hesitated. She just had to tell him no. Why couldn't she get that one little word out?

He watched her expectantly.

Maybe she could put it off for as long as possible. "Can we discuss it at the end of the summer?"

"We will one month wait. That is long enough." Without giving her a chance to contradict him, he bounded down the rest of the steps.

She pressed a hand to her forehead. She had to call after him and tell him that this was all a mistake. But as she opened her mouth, only a sigh of exasperation fell out.

She wasn't planning to marry Eric Meyer in one month no matter what he might think. Surely she'd find a way out of her predicament by then.

2

What was he doing in America?

Franz Meyer stepped off the Denver-Pacific Railroad into the busy fray of passengers coming and going on the platform outside the depot. Even though he knew he should keep going, he halted, forcing people to step around him.

Maybe he ought to get back on the train and return to Cheyenne and the Union Pacific that would take him back East.

As a fellow passed and jostled him, Franz steadied his hat and retreated a step so that he was almost plastered to the train car. He didn't belong in America. He didn't want to be in the uncivilized western town of Denver. And he certainly didn't want to ride up into the mountains where life was even more rustic and remote.

He peered to the west, the afternoon sky a brilliant and cloudless blue. He couldn't see the mountain range amidst the large buildings that surrounded the train depot, but he'd seen the peaks from his train car as he neared Denver. In May, snow still covered the summits, making them grander and more majestic than he'd imagined, going on for miles and miles from north to south.

Before leaving Germany, he'd briefly studied the geography and history of North America, and he'd learned that the Rocky Mountains started in Canada and spread across most of the western half of the United States. The presence of the mountain passes was what made traveling to California so difficult, especially before the transcontinental railroad was completed in 1869.

He'd read some of the tales of the early explorers and settlers, who'd used covered wagons to journey to the West. The trek had taken them weeks, even months.

Franz couldn't imagine how he would have endured such a trip. Four days on the train had been long enough.

Had Eric and Luisa gone by train? He imagined they probably would have, especially since she'd been with child.

The very thought of her carrying Eric's child sent a shaft of envy through Franz, as it always did. Perhaps the ache was a bit duller, like the stab of a blade that hadn't seen the whetstone in years and was growing rusty.

Still, the sting of the betrayal would never go away altogether.

Franz pressed a hand against his tweed coat and felt the crinkle of the paper and envelopes in his inner pocket, the four letters Eric had sent him over the past year. The first had come after Luisa's death, begging Franz for forgiveness. Eric had sent another several months later, pleading for forgiveness again and inviting him to visit. Two more had come only a few months ago in the spring.

The final letters had been decidedly different in nature, so much so that a strange worry had nagged Franz. It was a worry he hadn't liked and didn't want to feel, not after all that had happened. But Franz had sensed that Eric was in danger and was panicking, especially for his children.

In the last letter, Eric had asked Franz to take care of Dieter and Bianca if something ever happened to him. Eric had been worried the two children would be alone in the world without any support and would be taken to an orphanage.

Franz had wanted to say that it served Eric right for stealing his fiancée, that Eric had to live with the consequences of taking Luisa from him. Eric had been unforgivably selfish to gain her affection and woo her into sleeping with him, especially with the wedding plans underway. Then, of course, he'd gotten her pregnant and hadn't been able to hide the affair any longer.

Franz hadn't understood how Luisa could be more attracted to Eric. Although they both had light-brown hair and medium-blue eyes, Franz had always drawn the feminine attention more than his brother. Not only did he have sharper, more striking features, but he was more gregarious.

In the end, he simply hadn't been enough for Luisa.

As much as Franz resented Eric and Luisa and had vowed to cut himself off from them, he hadn't been able to ignore Eric's letters. At least, not for long. And here he was, on his way to visit his brother.

Franz blew out a breath and reached for the handle of the steps leading into the train car. Yes, he needed to get back on and go home to Berlin to his prestigious position at Friedrich-Wilhelms-Universität, to his friends, and to his comfortable apartment near the campus.

Of course, the university had given him the time off without any hesitation. He was, after all, one of their best professors. At twenty-eight, his youthfulness and his new methods of teaching attracted young and eager students from all over Deutschland and even beyond. The board of directors didn't want to lose him and had promised his job would be waiting upon his return.

Even so, he shouldn't have come to America, where he was only stirring up all the old feelings. Over the past six years since losing Luisa, he'd learned to be content. He'd made peace with not being married. And he'd decided he would remain a bachelor in order to devote all his time to his students.

Now, with each mile he drew closer to Eric, he could feel himself growing more unsettled. The angst inside was surfacing in a way that it hadn't in years. And the carefully crafted control of his life seemed to be slipping away.

He placed one foot onto the metal step leading to the train car, but his way was blocked by a young boy skipping down the stairs with his father and mother behind him.

"Hello, Professor Meyer." The boy with wavy blond hair and several missing front teeth smiled at him.

"Good day, Wilbur." Franz could speak English well enough that he'd had no trouble communicating so far. He'd studied languages during his own university days and was fluent in both French and English. He'd even spent one semester in England at Cambridge as a guest lecturer and had improved his English quite significantly then.

Wilbur had ridden in the seat across from him since changing trains in Cheyenne. The child had been talkative, and as soon as he'd learned Franz was a professor of history, geography, and philosophy, he'd bombarded him with questions for most of the journey.

Franz hadn't minded. After the weeks of traveling and being out of his classroom, he'd enjoyed the opportunity to engage with Wilbur, especially after learning he was six years old, the age of Eric and Luisa's firstborn child.

It had been fascinating to interact with the boy and to realize that Eric's son would likely act very much the same, perhaps even look similar.

Wilbur held out his hand. "You were coming back for this, weren't you?" The boy opened his fingers to reveal a gold chain holding two rings.

Franz lifted a hand to his neck to find that it was bare of the chain that he always wore.

A strange panic clamped around his chest, and he reached out for the rings, his fingers trembling as he took them from the boy. "Where did you find it?"

"It was on your seat," said Wilbur's mother, standing behind him and smiling down at her son.

Franz examined the chain, which had somehow snapped so that the links were broken. How had the rings stayed on? He was lucky they hadn't fallen off and rolled under the seats.

"These rings are very special to me." He closed his fist around them, his heart still pumping hard with strange panic. "I thank you for finding them."

The rings were more than special. They were his way of staying connected to his parents, and he'd worn the rings since the day their dead bodies had been returned to their family estate in Neubrandenburg.

He'd been sixteen and just getting ready to move to Berlin to attend university when the tragedy had happened. An assassin had attempted to take the life of the emperor. In the hail of gunfire, Vater had stepped in and taken the bullet. Unfortunately, Mutter, who had been at Vater's side, had also been shot.

Vater had become a national hero for saving the emperor, but the accolades and gifts and fame couldn't make up for the loss, and Franz had felt adrift without his parents for years. Sometimes he still felt as though he were on a ship at sea.

He moved off the train step to allow Wilbur and his parents to finish descending. He thanked them again and said another goodbye. But all the while, his mind was reeling with just how close he'd come to losing his parents' wedding bands.

As he stood next to the train and crushed the rings in his palm, his heart wouldn't stop thudding. The first thing he needed to do was find a jewelry shop and have the chain fixed or purchase a new one. He wouldn't be able to rest until it was done.

He slipped the rings into his trouser pocket, but even then, he couldn't pry his fingers loose. It was ridiculous, he knew, to feel so strongly about the rings. But he'd admired both of his parents more than anyone else. And the rings were a constant reminder of everything good, noble, and true that he wanted to become so that he could make them proud.

If they had been alive, they would have praised him for all he'd accomplished and the generous man that he was striving to be. They would have been proud of him . . . except for one thing—how he'd cut Eric out of his life.

At the blast of a train whistle, he released the rings and withdrew his hand from his pocket.

A heaviness settled over him, and he turned to face the west, where, somewhere in the wilderness, his brother was living with his two children.

For the past six years, Franz had tried to tell himself that the rings and the memories of his parents were all he had left of his family. But deep inside, he knew that wasn't true. He still had Eric and his two children. Franz could almost hear his parents telling him that he'd been a coward long enough and that it was past time to make peace with his brother.

Franz pushed away from the train and this time let the swell of people passing by move him along. As difficult as coming face-to-face again with Eric would be, he had to do it. He couldn't delay any longer.

3

"When will you marry Father?" Bianca's question pestered Clarabelle every bit as much as the gnats flying around them as they neared the lane that led to the Meyers' farm.

"He met with Mr. Irving, his solicitor, yesterday." Dieter was walking several steps ahead, swinging a stick like a sword and pretending to fight an imaginary dragon.

"What's a solicitor?" Bianca gripped Clarabelle's hand tightly, her steps slowing as if she weren't quite ready to let Clarabelle leave.

But the afternoon was waning, and Clarabelle had already lagged long enough after school waiting for the children to disperse. With Eric running late, she'd decided to walk Bianca and Dieter home. Now she needed to hurry to her family's ranch and assist with the chores. Even if her brother Maverick and his new wife Hazel had assured her that she should take all the time she needed at the school, Clarabelle still wanted to be of help.

Yes, she could admit, she also was anxious to be on her way because she didn't want to chance running into Eric.

Over the past three days since Eric had come to school and officially made his intentions known, she'd been dreading seeing him again. In fact, maybe she ought to wait on the road instead of accompanying the children down the lane to their door. She could watch them well enough from a distance without having to go all the way up to the cabin.

"A solicitor is a person who can marry Miss Oakley and Father." Dieter paused his pretend battle with the dragon to cast Bianca an exasperated look, as though she should have already known the answer to her question.

"The reverend is the one who does the marrying," Clarabelle corrected the young boy gently. "And the solicitor helps take care of the legal details of a marriage."

Dieter shrugged. "Either way, Father is ready to marry Miss Oakley."

Bianca tugged on Clarabelle's arm. "Father's ready, Miss Oakley." The girl repeated her brother's message as if, somehow, Clarabelle hadn't been able to hear the boy for herself.

Unfortunately, Clarabelle already knew Eric was ready. He'd made that very clear on Mrs. Grover's front porch. But as ready as Eric was, Clarabelle was far from ready or willing. Not even the past three days of trying to convince herself to go through with it had changed her mind.

Sunshine filtered through the newly budded leaves of the aspens that lined the lane leading to the Meyers' log cabin. She lifted her face, letting the light and warmth reach beyond the brim of her bonnet to bathe her skin. The air was warm, and the light felt especially good.

The outside of the home was well maintained. The logs were faded from years of weathering, but the chinking was solid. The place had real glass windows, a stone chimney on one end, and the front door and window shutters had been painted forest green.

The area surrounding the house had been cleared to make room for the strawberry and rhubarb patches that Luisa and Eric had cultivated. Over the past few years, they'd steadily increased their production so that they'd become one of the largest producers in the area.

Most of the Meyers' acreage, however, was devoted to growing hay. Even though in the high elevation they could usually only get in one hay cutting per year, the grass was sought after for its high nutritional value, and ranches—including High C Ranch—were willing to pay a premium for the locally grown hay.

"Maybe you can marry Father tonight," Bianca persisted, "since he's ready. Then you can move in and start living with us."

"We can help you." Dieter turned around now completely and was peering up at her with his serious gaze. "We'll go over to your home right now, pack your bags, and bring all your stuff over."

Bianca nodded. "I'm very strong now that I'm five, and I can carry heavy bags."

Clarabelle's slow amble came to a halt, her mare nudging her from behind and then nickering, as if to complain.

She had to say something to correct the children regarding marriage to their father. She couldn't allow them to think she would go through with it. But how could she disappoint them when they were so obviously excited about having a new mother?

"You'll make Father happy." Dieter's eyes held a sadness that Clarabelle had seen there more and more often lately. Was he worried about his father? Maybe he wanted his father to have a new wife more than he wanted a new mother.

"I think you'll like sleeping with Father," Bianca said as solemnly as Dieter.

"Oh dear." The girl's comment was likely innocent, and she probably didn't mean to insinuate anything, but heat flared into Clarabelle's cheeks anyway. "We mustn't talk that way, sweetie."

"It's true," Dieter added. "Mutti loved snuggling—"

"Even so, it's not polite to talk about fathers and

mothers sleeping together."

"It's not?" Bianca's eyes widened.

What happened in the bedroom between married couples was certainly not anything to talk about, much less think about, which had been difficult over the past weeks since Maverick had married Hazel and they often disappeared into their bedroom at all hours of the day.

When they weren't in their bedroom, they couldn't keep their hands off each other, and Clarabelle had lost count of how many times she'd come upon them and found them kissing.

She loved seeing them so happy together and thought they were undeniably romantic. Their love was tangible— so much so that it made Clarabelle all the more certain that was the kind of love she wanted some day: the kind her parents had always shared, the kind that was so deep and selfless that nothing else compared.

Which meant she couldn't marry Eric. She absolutely couldn't.

She needed—passionately wanted—to love and be loved so thoroughly that she wouldn't be able to keep her hands off her husband or vice versa. She wanted others to lose track of how much she and her husband kissed. And she wanted to disappear with him into their bedroom.

If that kind of romance could happen for others, it could happen for her too. At least, she hoped so.

But for now, in front of Bianca and Dieter, such

notions were best left unspoken. Instead, she had to let them know she wouldn't be sharing a bed with their father—not to sleep or to snuggle. "I know you want your father to be happy, but—"

"He likes you a lot, Miss Oakley." Dieter was watching her face as though he was reading all her thoughts. "He said you're very pretty and kind."

Very pretty and kind. Well, that was something. The compliment was flattering, especially because Clementine was the one who usually drew the attention from the men, along with the compliments.

Men were always more attracted to her bubbliness, laughter, and friendliness. She was lively and knew how to have fun, and the fellows liked that better than Clarabelle's serious, reasonable nature.

"He wants to marry you very much," Dieter continued. "And he'll make you happy, too, if you give him a chance."

The child was persuasive. If Clarabelle wasn't careful, she'd find herself giving in to him the same way she had to Eric.

She opened her mouth, trying to find the words to respond. But before she could say anything, Bianca tugged on her arm while pointing down the lane in the direction of the strawberry patch where the plants were beginning to flower. "Look, Father is sleeping."

Dieter followed his sister's finger and then frowned.

Bianca glanced up at Clarabelle with remorseful eyes. "I'm sorry, Miss Oakley. I shouldn't have said *sleeping* since it's not polite."

"You should have said *resting*." Dieter sounded like he was sixteen instead of six. "Or *slumbering*. Right, Miss Oakley?"

"I didn't mean that you couldn't ever use the word *sleeping*." Clarabelle's mind scrambled for a way to explain what she'd really meant in regards to marital intimacy. But as her gaze found Eric in the strawberry patch, her every thought came to an abrupt halt.

He was lying face down in the dirt, one arm stretched above his head, the other bent at an awkward angle at his side. He wasn't sleeping. Or resting. Or slumbering. No, he'd clearly keeled over and appeared to be unconscious.

She tossed the reins of her horse around the nearest tree branch, then she started running down the lane toward him, her heart drumming an ominous warning with each step she took.

When she reached the field, she tried to dodge the fragile strawberry plants. She didn't want to crush any of them or the flowers and ruin the hard work the Meyers had put into their strawberry crop. But urgency propelled her, so that by the time she dropped to his side, she was nearly frantic.

"Eric." She shook his shoulder, praying he'd rouse and push up and be all right.

But he didn't budge.

She shook him again, this time more forcefully. "Eric. Wake up."

He lay absolutely still and silent.

The children were at the edge of the strawberry field now, having raced after her.

She held up a hand to them. "Wait there."

Bianca stopped right away, but Dieter bounded into the field.

Clarabelle hefted Eric, trying to roll him over. As she did so, she saw the blood—lots of it on his temple.

Oh, sweet heavens. He was injured.

"Dieter, stop." This time her voice was commanding enough that it halted the boy in his steps. His breathing was labored from running, just like hers was, and his eyes were wild, as if he knew something was terribly wrong.

She had to say something to him. "Your father is injured."

"How badly?" The boy's voice shook.

She tried to roll Eric again, and this time she managed to get him on his side. His eyes were closed, and dark blood ran from his head, matting his hair, smearing his forehead, and causing soil to stick to his face.

She searched for the source of the blood and found a long, deep gash just beyond his hairline. The flesh was split open, and his skull was indented, as if he'd taken quite a blow. The oozing wound was ghastly, but she had to do something for him—if he were even still alive.

She pressed her fingers against his neck and mouth, searching for a pulse and for breathing, but she couldn't feel any signs of life.

"He has an injury on his head." She tried to keep her voice calm so that she wouldn't worry the children more than they already were. "Dieter, take my horse and ride back into town. Go straight to the doctor's office or his house and tell him that your father's been injured."

She knew the boy could ride well. Since they still had a couple hours of daylight left, he'd be able to accomplish the task.

He hesitated.

"Hurry now."

Dieter gave a nod, then began to run back to where she'd left her horse.

"Bianca, I need you to go into the house and bring me some rags and clean water."

Bianca was staring at her father's bloody face, her lips wobbling.

"You'd like me to wash up your father's face, wouldn't you?"

She nodded.

"Then do as I've instructed and bring me rags and water."

Bianca scampered away too.

As soon as the children were far enough away,

Clarabelle laid her hand against Eric's chest and willed his heart to beat.

But the only thing that beat a rhythm was his declaration from a few days ago: *"I fear for mine safety."*

She scanned the cleared fields that surrounded the cabin.

Beyond the strawberry patch, sunlight glinted off the hay that had already begun to grow and turn green. A scraggly woodland lay in the distance beyond the fields, gradually rising into the hills and rocky slopes of the Front Range Mountains that separated the high country from Denver.

She didn't see anyone or anything unusual, but fear prickled at the back of her neck. The people who'd brutally attacked Eric were still out there.

The question was, why had they hurt Eric? More questions quickly followed: Would they strike again? And who would they hurt next time?

4

"Mr. Meyer is dead." Dr. Howell spoke solemnly from beside Eric's bed. The smattering of gray hair upon his head was sticking straight up, adding a couple of inches to his small frame.

Even though Clarabelle had suspected Eric was dead from the moment she'd found him in the field, the proclamation still sent a sharp pang through her chest.

"There's nothing you can do?" Maverick stood beside Clarabelle on the side of the bed opposite the doctor, Eric's body laid out before them.

"From what I can tell, he's been dead for a while." The older fellow spoke in a low whisper, casting a glance to the closed bedroom door.

With the children in the front room of the cabin with Hazel and Clementine, Clarabelle was glad the doctor was being sensitive with how loudly he spoke. The situation was horrific enough for Bianca and Dieter, and they didn't need to hear all the particulars.

The news of Eric's attack and injury had obviously spread, because Reverend Livingston and Mr. and Mrs. Grover were also in the other room. Like Clarabelle, they'd all been holding out hope that somehow Eric would regain consciousness and perhaps be able to tell them what had happened and who was to blame. But now they might never know.

Clarabelle leaned into Maverick, needing his strength to hold her up as the reality of the situation sank in.

Maverick slipped his arm around her. Thankfully, Dieter had gone to High C Ranch first before heading to town. It hadn't taken long for Maverick to show up at the Meyers' cabin, and he'd helped Clarabelle carry Eric inside.

Now Dr. Howell folded up his stethoscope and slipped it back into his leather doctor's bag. "I'm sorry. I wish there were more we could do, but the trauma from the blow likely killed him on impact."

"Then he was murdered." Maverick's tone was low and grave.

"It's obvious someone hit him with a hard object," the doctor replied. "But it's more difficult to assess whether the person intended to outright kill Eric or only injure him."

"Reckon there's been foul play either way." Maverick had discarded his Stetson, and his dark hair was messy.

His denims and flannel shirt were dusty and held the scent of horses and hay. "I oughta go fetch the sheriff."

The small bedroom had only enough room for the double bed, the trunk along the far wall, and a leveled tree stump next to the bed that served as a table to hold the lantern. A small mirror graced one of the log walls, but otherwise the room was plain and simple, devoid of anything that might give the place a homey touch.

Now that the darkness of evening had fallen, the lantern illuminated Eric's pale face that she'd washed clean of the soil and blood. The bandage she'd pressed to his wound was loosely in place.

But it didn't matter anymore. Eric was gone, and his children were now orphans without either a father or mother or any other relatives who would be willing to take them in and provide for them.

She'd reassured Eric earlier in the week that she would help with the children if anything happened to him, but what right did she have if she wasn't legally their mother? Now what would become of them? The land? The cabin?

She certainly had no intention of abandoning them in their moment of greatest need and would do everything she could to help them. She had a good example from her parents in having an open heart and open home. After all, they'd taken in two homeless orphans—her brothers Ryder and Tanner—during the wagon train ride west to Colorado.

But she was a single woman without a means to support herself, much less two children. No doubt Maverick would be open to her bringing them back to High C Ranch to live there, but they weren't his responsibility.

First, before any of that, they had to tell the children that their father was dead.

As Dr. Howell made his way around the bed toward the door, she released a sigh.

"You doing all right?" Maverick asked, his eyes alight with compassion.

"I'm not relishing having to give the news to the children."

"We'll do it together."

A soft tap on the bedroom door was followed by its opening a crack, forcing Dr. Howell to take a step back. A middle-aged gentleman poked his head inside. The narrow face with a perpetually serious expression belonged to Mr. Irving, Breckenridge's only attorney. With his long sideburns, bushy beard, and top hat, he reminded her of a picture she'd once seen of former president Abraham Lincoln.

"May I come in?" Mr. Irving's gaze darted to the bed and Eric's lifeless form.

Maverick nodded. "Might as well."

Mr. Irving had handled their family's affairs not only after Pa had died but also recently, with Ma's passing, reading the will and transferring the deed of the ranch to Maverick.

The slender man slipped into the room. Before he could close the door, Mr. Grover pushed his way inside. Next to Mr. Irving's thin and tall frame, Mr. Grover was much shorter and stouter, with a fleshy face devoid of any facial hair.

As he closed the door, Clarabelle had to flatten herself against the log wall to make room for the newcomers in the tiny space. Even then, they all stood rather stiffly together in front of the bed.

Mr. Grover visibly blanched at the sight of Eric. "What's the prognosis, doctor?"

The doctor shook his head sadly. "Unfortunately, he didn't survive the injury."

Mr. Irving leveled his severe gaze upon Clarabelle. "As your fiancé, Mr. Meyer gave you everything, including the children."

He wasn't her fiancé.

As the eyes of each of the men shifted to her, including Maverick's surprised gaze, Clarabelle wished a portal would magically open and allow her to escape.

But the gazes upon her didn't waver, and she was stuck under the weight of them.

Maverick was the first to speak. "You didn't tell us you got engaged."

"Eric proposed to her three days ago," Mr. Irving

answered before Clarabelle could offer an explanation. "He said they were planning to get married very soon. He'd hoped within a few weeks."

"Is that true?" Maverick's brows rose.

Clarabelle swallowed her rising panic. Eric might have been making plans, but she hadn't agreed to anything. How could she clarify the misunderstanding with all the men staring at her?

"Well?" Maverick persisted.

"He did propose." She hesitated, trying to find a plausible explanation. "But we didn't make any solid plans."

"They were apparently solid enough for Eric." Mr. Irving pulled an official-looking paper out of his inner coat pocket. "He had me draw up his Last Will and Testament and named you as his only beneficiary."

For heaven's sake. Could this situation get any worse?

The only good thing was that at least she could take care of Bianca and Dieter without anyone questioning her right to do so. Not that she planned to be with them forever, but after all that Ryder and Tanner had gone through as orphans and living in orphanages before running away, she could hopefully spare Bianca and Dieter more upheaval and heartache than they were already bound to feel.

"I didn't know you were interested in Eric Meyer." Maverick was now searching her face, as if looking for the same love and adoration that he had for Hazel. Her brother could search forever and wouldn't find it.

But at the moment, she was too embarrassed to admit it in front of everyone. Instead, she gave what she hoped was a nonchalant shrug. "He was looking for a mother for his children."

"Hazel said he approached you about it at Ma's funeral, but I told her you wouldn't want to marry a man you didn't love."

"Some people get married for convenience," Mr. Irving interjected. "I've seen it happen plenty of times, especially here in the West."

Mr. Grover was stroking his gold watch chain. "I'll admit that's how Mrs. Grover and I got our start."

Dr. Howell nodded as though he'd seen marriages of convenience a million times over and there was nothing to it.

But Clarabelle wanted more to it. Love. And she still wasn't willing to give up her dream of having a man who was so in love with her that he'd do anything to be with her.

"It's neither here nor there now." Mr. Irving unfolded the will and handed it to Maverick. Clarabelle bit back her irritation that the gentleman hadn't given the document to her first, as though she wasn't smart enough to read it for herself.

Mr. Irving pointed to a section of the will. "You'll see

here that Eric even gave Clarabelle access to his bank account. He didn't disclose his financial situation, but he said he'd make sure there was enough so that she wouldn't have to struggle."

Mr. Grover leaned forward, straining to see the will.

The doctor, on the other hand, stifled a yawn, the exhaustion on his face a testament to the strenuous nature of his work at all hours of the day and night.

He needed to be on his way. And she needed to speak to the children. She would have plenty of time later to sort out Eric's will and financial situation. "At least for the time being, the children and I can live here until I can figure out what we'll do." Hopefully the money Eric had in the bank would carry her over for a few weeks. If she were lucky, maybe it would see her and the children through the summer.

Maverick frowned. "You can't stay here. Not alone."

"I concur," Mr. Grover said as though the matter were settled. "A woman cannot manage a spread like this without a man."

Irritation flared to life again inside Clarabelle. She didn't consider herself to be a suffragist or feminist or whatever the title was for women who wanted more rights, but she hadn't realized just how few women were truly independent the way men were. If Eric had been able to live on his own with just the children, why couldn't she? Why did men have a double standard when the roles were reversed?

Maverick shook his head at Mr. Grover. "I'm not doubting Clarabelle's capability to manage the Meyers' spread. She's a hard worker, and we'll pitch in and help."

Clarabelle offered her brother a smile of gratitude for his confidence in her.

"What I'm worried about is her safety," Maverick continued. "With a killer on the loose, I don't want her staying here alone and being in danger."

Everyone fell silent.

Maverick did have a good point. Until they learned who had murdered Eric, they had to be cautious.

Ever since she'd found Eric in the field, she'd been trying to figure out who might have hurt him. With the way he'd been worried during the past week, she'd concluded that the killer hadn't been a random stranger passing by. Someone he'd known had caused him to be concerned. Or something had happened to make him think he was in danger. But who or what?

All of that had nothing to do with her. In fact, Eric had seemed confident she'd be fine taking care of his children. "I must stay here for now to tend to the livestock and crops. And the children need the stability. They've lost their mother and father. It wouldn't be fair for them to lose their home too."

As soon as she spoke the words, she knew Maverick would understand. They'd lost their pa and ma in short succession. It would have been even more devastating if they'd been forced from the place they loved and had to learn to start over and fend for themselves somewhere new.

Maverick studied her face, then nodded. "All right. But I'll give you Pa's pistol, and you'll need to promise to wear it at all times."

"I promise."

"And if there's any sign of danger, you'll come straight over to the ranch?"

"I will."

"In the meantime," Mr. Irving cut into the conversation, "we'll be doing our best to find Clarabelle a husband who can take over the spread and help raise the children."

"I agree," Mr. Grover said as he began to open the door and put an end to the conversation. "Clarabelle needs a husband. The sooner she's married, the better."

As the men began to file out of the bedroom, Clarabelle wished she had the ability to stand up for herself. But as always, the protest lodged in her throat. She could only pray everything would work out for the best.

5

Franz slowed his steps as a cabin came into view. The morning sunlight was shining on the rustic log structure, as if pointing a finger to direct him there.

It had to be Eric's home.

Franz pulled the third of Eric's four letters out of his pocket, then perched his spectacles upon his nose and skimmed the letter to the part where Eric had described his little farm just north of Breckenridge.

A log cabin set back from the road. Stone chimney. Two front windows made of glass. Door and shutters painted green.

Yes, everything was just as Eric had described.

Franz folded the paper, tucked it back into his pocket, then frowned at the home.

Why had Eric been happy with such a hovel, no bigger than the peasant cottages on the land their family had owned for generations in and around Neubrandenburg?

How could Eric be proud of a house made of logs when he'd grown up in a castle on Lake Tollensesee? Made of stones quarried in the area, the family estate had a grandeur and history that had drawn even the emperor for a visit once when he and Eric had been boys.

Franz pocketed his spectacles, released a sigh, and continued on the wagon path he'd been following since leaving town.

He'd arrived by stagecoach late the previous evening. Even though darkness had fallen, the light coming from the windows of homes and businesses had illuminated the wide main thoroughfare enough for him to see that the town was just as simple and ramshackle as he'd been told.

Stumps littered the landscape where trees had been cut down to make room for more construction projects. Canvas tents and log structures intermingled with buildings mostly made of wood, many of them with false fronts, which was apparently a way to make them look bigger and more important than they really were.

Spirited music had spilled out of the open doors of saloons and dance halls, and the streets were busy at the evening hour with men loitering on boardwalks, laughing and talking and smoking cigars.

Franz had gone straight to the nearest hotel, purchased a meal, then taken a private room. Although he'd partly wanted to go right away to Eric's home and show himself, another part had hung back—the same part that had delayed him in Denver for the past week.

He pressed his hand against his starched shirt, feeling the outline of a new chain and the two rings back where he'd worn them for years—right near his heart. He'd found the best jeweler in Denver and commissioned a new chain, which had taken more time than he'd anticipated.

Then one evening while dining at his hotel, he'd recognized an older couple who had been friends with his parents and the family. They now lived in New York City but were on vacation in Denver. They'd convinced him to join them for several of their excursions around the city including the theater, opera, and gardens.

Since he wanted to make the most of his time in the United States and in seeing all the sights that he'd only read about, he hadn't minded postponing his departure. During one of their last outings, when the older couple had paired him with a young lady—a friend of a friend— he'd decided it was finally time to leave Denver. Not only hadn't he wanted to spend time with any marriageable young women, but he also had to do what he'd come for.

Franz halted at a dirt path that wound through overlong grass and shrubs and aspens to the cabin. His stomach gave a lurch. This was it. The moment he'd been thinking about since the day he'd boarded the steamship in Hamburg more than a month ago. He was about to see his brother after six years apart.

What would they have to say to each other?

Franz pushed down his trepidation and forced his feet to start down the lane.

The place was quiet, almost as if no one were home or even living there anymore. Though a crisp morning breeze whispered among the long blades of grass, there wasn't movement anywhere else, except a lone hen to one side of the cabin, pecking the earth.

Eric had said that he made a living by growing crops, mostly specializing in hay. The cleared fields beyond the cabin attested to those crops.

Franz paused and let his gaze sweep over the cabin and fields and the mountains rising in the distance beyond. Taken as a whole, he could admit the land was beautiful here, more so than he'd expected.

In fact, during the stagecoach ride up Boreas Pass, he'd enjoyed the view of the snow-covered peaks as they'd loomed larger than life. He'd seen several moose, elk, and even a black bear fishing along a riverbank. When they'd reached the summit of the pass, they'd driven by heaping mounds of snow that hadn't yet melted even though the first day of June had been upon them.

He supposed he could understand to some degree why Eric had chosen this area to build a new life. Not only was it breathtaking, but it was far away from the gossip and loathing and shunning that Eric and Luisa had earned from friends and family for all that had happened.

At the crack of a branch nearby, the hairs on the back of Franz's neck stood up with the premonition that someone was watching him. He scanned both sides of the dirt path, but only small butterflies and other insects fluttered about the grass.

Franz straightened his shoulders with resolve, then strode onward down the path.

"Now!" came a loud whisper from the trees.

A moment later, something began to fall above him. He glanced up in time to see what appeared to be a blanket before it landed upon his face and over his body.

"We got him!" came a boy's excited shout from a nearby tree.

"Help me down, Dieter," said a little girl from another tree.

"I'm coming. But first I need to secure our prisoner."

At the thump of feet hitting the ground and the crackle of brush, Franz guessed the boy had launched himself down from the tree. Dieter was the name of Eric's boy. Which meant the girl was Bianca. Eric had talked about both in his letters.

Were they playing some sort of game with him? Should he toss off the blanket or should he allow them to pretend that they really had captured him as their prisoner?

"Do you think he's the killer?" The little girl's voice contained a note of fear.

"He has to be. Why else would he be here?"

Their English was impeccable, without a trace of a German accent. Clearly, Eric and Luisa had wanted their children to be seen as Americans and not Germans— likely because of the discrimination German immigrants often faced, if the stories were true.

Little hands grabbed at the blanket that barely covered Franz's head and chest. "Don't move, mister," the boy said as he yanked the blanket tighter only to pull it halfway off Franz.

Franz held himself motionless. "Like this?"

"Yes, just like that."

The boy found Franz's arms and tugged first one behind his back and then the other. A second later, he began to wind a rope around Franz's wrists.

"Dieter? What's wrong?" A woman's worried call came from the direction of the cabin—or at least, what sounded like that direction, since Franz couldn't see with the blanket draped over his head and covering his face.

"We captured the killer!" Dieter yelled back, excitement still lacing his voice.

"Dieter!" This time the woman's voice was laced with rebuke more than worry. "You can't capture anyone. It's not safe."

The slap of footsteps told Franz the woman was hurrying their way. Who was she? Had Eric remarried? He hadn't mentioned a new wife in any of his letters, but perhaps he'd married again over recent months. It wouldn't surprise Franz. He could only imagine the difficulty in raising two young children without a helpmate.

Dieter's fingers fumbled with the rope, and it slipped away. But Franz kept his arms where the boy had positioned them, and a moment later, Dieter was wrapping the rope around Franz's wrists again. "I'm almost done securing him, then I'll ride into town for the sheriff."

Franz almost smiled. The boy was taking his playtime rather seriously to suggest going after the sheriff.

"Clarabelle, I need help down," the little girl pleaded.

"Oh, sweetie." The woman—presumably named Clarabelle—was surely exasperated by the antics of the children, but she obviously had a patient temperament. Beneath the blanket covering his head, he could see her skirt now, a simple green calico, along with a pair of boots. She approached the tree beside Franz and seemed to be lifting the girl into her arms.

"I told you that we don't have anything to worry about." Her tone was gentle and filled with compassion.

"I'm just doing my part," Dieter said, "like Maverick told me to do."

"It is noble, I will agree," Franz interjected, guessing it was past time for him to speak and make his introductions. Eric was likely to come check on his family at any moment, and Franz wanted to be ready. "Although, I would be happy to give you instructions for how to form a more secure knot." Or any knot at all, for that matter.

Franz had hardly spoken anything but English since arriving in America. Even so, his German accent was still strong. At the sound of it, the woman tugged the blanket off Franz's head, taking his hat with it.

He found himself peering at a lovely young woman with blond hair containing a slight auburn tint. She wore her hair in a long single braid that hung over one shoulder, and her head was topped with a cowboy's hat. He'd seen enough of them during his journey to know.

Her face was pale and unblemished, making her green eyes startlingly clear and bright. Her expression was indeed filled with patience and compassion, confirming that she was undoubtedly a good mother to Eric's two children.

Clarabelle. She had a pretty name.

His gaze slid down. It couldn't seem to help itself. Not when the little girl's hold seemed to plaster Clarabelle's bodice and skirt to a body with curves in all the right places. Perfect proportions, a slender waist, defined hips, and long legs.

She was the opposite of Luisa, who'd been dark-haired, short, and dainty.

Perhaps Eric had chosen someone completely

different so that he didn't have to compare the two. Maybe having opposite wives would make a second marriage easier.

Franz knew he was ogling her, but she seemed to be taking him in with just as much interest. Well, maybe not quite as much, since his ogling resembled that of a gangly adolescent boy who was face-to-face with the most beautiful girl in the neighborhood.

She cocked her head, her elegant brows rising and revealing shy eyes.

For several heartbeats, Franz lost himself in those eyes, longing swelling in waves. He had a strangely visceral need for her, one that involved pulling her into his arms, holding her close, and getting to experience everything about her.

He was shocked at the heat that rippled through him . . . and the lust. He hadn't had such a strong reaction to a woman in years—maybe not ever. Certainly, he'd loved Luisa and had been attracted to her, but the need had never been so strong or so urgent.

He took a rapid step backward, bumping into the boy, who was still trying to tie a knot in the rope binding his wrists. Franz wanted to blame his reaction on the fact that he'd been celibate for so many years and that he'd avoided interacting with women to keep himself in check. But he'd just spent time with the friend-of-a-friend woman in Denver and hadn't felt this kind of desire.

Clarabelle's gaze was trailing around his face. "You wouldn't happen to be Eric's brother, would you?"

For just a fraction of an instant, he wanted to deny it—steal this woman away from his brother and hurt Eric in equal measure. But Franz rapidly shook his head. He'd never, ever do it. Not only did he want to do what was right, but he'd come to apologize, not seek revenge.

"Oh." She uttered the one word with a huff of breath that contained her disappointment. "I'm sorry. It's just that you look so much like Eric."

"Yes, I am."

Her brows furrowed with confusion.

He was acting like he'd lost his mind around this woman. Maybe he had. "Now it is my turn to apologize. I am Eric's brother. My name is Franz."

Behind him, Dieter froze.

"You're his brother from Germany?" she asked again, seemingly less to query him than to convince herself.

"I am he. I came to Breckenridge last night on the stagecoach."

Dieter let go of the rope, and it fell to the ground. But he didn't seem to care anymore. Instead, he sidled around and peered up at Franz.

At the sight of the boy's face, so much like Eric's, a vise clamped onto Franz's chest. "You must be Dieter. And you"—he took in the little girl, who was now resting her head on the woman's shoulder—"must be Bianca."

With her dark hair and petite features, the girl resembled Luisa so much that he could almost feel her presence and hear her voice. This child—both children—could have been Luisa's and his. He would have been the one with the family and the full life.

Instead, Eric had gotten everything that should have been his.

Dieter was examining him with wide blue eyes that were so much like his and Eric's. "You're my uncle?"

Franz swallowed the sorrow that had so quickly surfaced. "Yes, I am." If the family resemblance wasn't enough, he had a photograph to prove it. He dug into his coat pocket, found the worn picture among the letters, and pulled it out.

"Here." He held it out, revealing himself and Eric standing together along the shore of Lake Tollensesee, taken the autumn he'd left for the university. The two of them stood side by side, arms slung over each other's shoulders, both with their light brown hair, youthful faces, and bright smiles. Little had they known how much would change in a few short months.

Dieter studied the photo. "That is Father." He made the pronouncement as if the matter were settled and he could finally trust Franz.

Even so, Franz held out the picture to Clarabelle and Bianca.

They bent their heads and examined the picture too.

"Uncle Franz." Dieter's voice seemed to hold both welcome and excitement. At least, Franz hoped so.

Clarabelle glanced from the picture to him and back. "You don't need to convince me. It's obvious enough."

"It has been a while, and I am sure we have both changed." Franz peered down the lane, his gut cinching. Would Eric welcome him just as openly as his children? And his wife?

Bianca wiggled to free herself from Clarabelle. The movement only tightened Clarabelle's garments more snuggly to her body, accentuating her generous curves once again.

He dragged his gaze—and his thoughts—away from those generous curves and focused on her face. She had such pretty cheekbones that angled down to a slender jaw and chin. And her mouth and lips had a full curve that no doubt made her very kissable.

Bianca shuffled so that she was standing beside her brother. "Does this mean we don't need to go get the sheriff?"

"Uncle Franz will keep us safe now." Dieter glanced around as if he really did expect a killer to jump out from behind the nearest tree. "Won't you, Uncle Franz?"

Franz nodded. "Of course I will."

"Now children," Clarabelle said gently. "We don't need to live in fear."

"But the killer is still out there," Dieter said.

Something wasn't quite right. What if Eric and his family were in danger? Was it possible Dieter hadn't been playing when he'd thrown the blanket?

Franz surveyed the landscape again. Surely if Eric were home, he would have heard the commotion the same way Clarabelle had, and he would have come to investigate by now. "Is Eric gone?"

Having opened her mouth to respond to Dieter, Clarabelle paused, her gaze swinging to Franz and her eyes brimming with compassion. "I'm so sorry, Franz. But yes, he's gone."

He wasn't sure whether to feel relieved or disappointed that Eric wouldn't be rushing out to greet him. Maybe the delay would give him a chance to be more prepared for what to say. "When will he be back?"

"Back?" Clarabelle's brow furrowed.

"Yes, did he say when he would return?"

For a moment, everyone looked at him as if he'd sprouted long ears and a tail and turned into a donkey.

Then Clarabelle shuddered and hugged her arms together. "It's not like that," she whispered. "He won't be coming back . . . because he's dead."

6

Dead?

Franz tried to let the word penetrate his mind, but it only seemed to bounce off.

Eric couldn't be dead. He was young and healthy and happy with his new life in America, here in Colorado.

But even as Franz denied the possibility of Eric's death, he only had to glance at the faces of Eric's family to realize the truth.

His brother *was* dead.

A strange hollow emptiness inside him echoed with the realization. Franz was ashamed to admit that in those early months following Eric's betrayal, he'd sometimes hoped Eric would have hardships and that God would punish him for what he'd done.

But he'd never wished death upon Eric.

He met Clarabelle's gaze. "How long ago?"

"One week." As she hugged herself, this time he

noticed the gun belt around her waist and the pistol holstered at her side. Did all women in the area wear guns, or was she carrying one because Dieter hadn't been playing when he'd said that a killer was still out there?

"What happened?"

"Father was murdered." Dieter offered the news solemnly before Clarabelle could speak.

Bianca's face was just as grave. "The bad guy hit him on the head."

Clarabelle was gazing off to one of the fields beyond the cabin, and her eyes held a faraway look, as if she was reliving all that had happened.

He was tempted to feel sorry for himself for coming all the way to Colorado and failing in his mission to see Eric and restore a semblance of peace. But his predicament was nothing compared to the children and Clarabelle's and all they'd experienced. If Eric really had been murdered, then it must have been traumatic—likely still was traumatic.

Even though he didn't know the first thing about Eric's new wife—other than that he was drawn to her—he could only imagine just how hard it would be to marry a man only to lose him and then have to raise his children.

She seemed to shake herself out of the past and waved him forward. "Where are my manners? My name is Clarabelle. Please. You must come in. I'll start a fresh pot of coffee."

He couldn't resist the invitation. He needed to hear all the details of what had happened to Eric. And he wanted the chance to get to know the children and Clarabelle.

He walked with them down the rest of the lane. When he ducked inside the cabin, he was surprised at how clean and orderly the interior was. It had a main front room with a table and benches, corner stove, and a small sitting area with a sofa and two chairs. A bedroom branched off the back of the house, and a loft opened up above where he guessed the children slept.

Franz took a seat at the table, and the children sat on either side of him while Clarabelle brewed coffee. Between the three of them, he was able to piece together the full story of Eric's attack in the strawberry patch and how they'd found him lifeless. The funeral had been five days ago, and now they were trying to adjust to not having Eric.

A strange sense of grief and regret settled inside Franz. Although Clarabelle seemed sad about everything, she didn't seem to be grieving too greatly. It confirmed his suspicion that his brother had only been married a short time and that perhaps the marriage had even been born out of a need for a mother for the children. Certainly, Clarabelle did care for them. It was evident in how she interacted and spoke to them that she was a good mother.

But the longer he talked with them, the more

burdened he felt. How would she be able to provide for herself? She couldn't possibly manage the hay and other crops and all the other work involved in trying to eke out a living while at the same time being able to properly take care of the children.

In addition to worries about Eric's family, Franz also needed time to sort through all that had happened to Eric and what he ought to do about it. Apparently the sheriff had investigated the murder as much as he could, but without finding any evidence or even any motivation, the sheriff didn't know where to begin searching for the killer.

Franz was grateful he didn't have to rush back to Germany and his teaching position. When he'd taken the leave of absence, he hadn't specified a return date, hadn't known how long he'd want to stay in Colorado. He guessed he'd been waiting to find out how Eric would receive him. He'd hoped Eric would be happy to see him, but he hadn't known exactly how things would go.

The truth was, he could stay for a while in Summit County and make sure Clarabelle and the children were secure. At the same time, maybe he could do some probing of his own to find out more about why Eric had been murdered.

"Thank you," he said as Clarabelle refilled his mug.

The children had finally tired of all the talking and had moved out of the house, into the front grassy area to play where Clarabelle could watch them through the windows and open front door.

Franz knew he needed to go, that he'd likely overstayed his welcome. Clarabelle probably had a dozen tasks requiring her attention and didn't need him there distracting her from her work. But he hadn't been able to make himself get up from the table.

Somehow, being in Eric's home, sitting there and sipping coffee, he could almost feel connected to his brother again. At the very least, he could picture Eric's life in America in a way he'd never been able to do before. The life hadn't been easy and had been so different from the luxury and ease they'd known growing up, but from what Franz could tell, Eric had been happy and had loved living here.

As Clarabelle returned the coffee pot to the stove, he followed her every move, all too aware of how her presence in the house seemed to light it up more than the sunshine coming in through the windows.

Even from behind, she was much too attractive, with her braid hanging down her back drawing attention to her gracefulness, her slender waist, and her perfectly rounded backside.

When she reached the bench across from him, she halted and brushed at her skirt, clearly sensing his scrutiny. "I'm sorry I'm not more put together today. If I'd known you were coming, I would have taken more care to be presentable."

During the whole visit, all he'd been able to think was that she was incredibly beautiful without even trying or knowing. And a small part of him had been jealous of Eric again. What did Eric have that he could so easily win not only Luisa but now Clarabelle?

She lowered herself to the bench and picked up her coffee, her eyes once again on the children outside—those stunning green eyes.

"How long were you and Eric married?" The question was blunt, but he couldn't help himself. He wanted to know more about her.

She nearly dropped her coffee mug to the table, the liquid sloshing over the rim and onto her hand. She drew in a hissing breath, likely from the coffee burning her skin. She immediately lifted her hand to her lips and pressed the affected area to her mouth.

Her lips and mouth on her skin.

That same heat as before shot through him—the heat that pumped his blood with need he hadn't experienced in far too long.

It was wrong to think of wanting her. She was his brother's widow—a brother who'd been deceased for only a week. Even so, Franz's attraction to her went beyond rationalization. And yes, he prided himself on being a rational man.

He was logical, using both deductive and inductive reasoning to make arguments, using syllogisms to make inferences, and using mathematical equations and symbols to prove theories. He was thorough and analytical. And he had several degrees and could teach on just about any subject.

But at this moment, with this woman, everything he'd ever learned and known seemed to abandon him, leaving his mind empty of all coherent thoughts.

As she lowered her hand and he glimpsed the red burnt spot on her skin, he silently cursed himself. Hastily he pushed back from the table and rose. He stalked over to the side table, where she'd left a pitcher of water. He grabbed the closest rag, poured water onto it, and then returned to the table.

"Here." He reached for her hand.

She hesitated, keeping her gaze averted from his.

"Please." He gentled his tone.

She held it out.

As he touched her hand, his pulse raced forward erratically. Why was he having this kind of reaction to her? He didn't know her, had just met her, and shouldn't be so attracted to her already. But he was. There was no denying it.

Was this what love at first sight felt like? He'd never believed in it—thought it was for fairy tales. Yes, a person could feel attraction right away. But not love. Not with someone they didn't know.

But had he been wrong?

Eric had claimed his attraction to Luisa had been strong and instantaneous, and Franz had scoffed at him. What if Eric really had felt a magnetism?

It didn't excuse the cheating and everything that had happened, but maybe Eric and Luisa had experienced more chemistry together than Franz had realized was conceivable because he'd never felt it before . . . until now.

He placed the cold, wet rag on Clarabelle's red skin. "That should help."

"Thank you." She reached for the rag, as though intending to take it from him and hold it on her own.

But he didn't relinquish it, wasn't ready to let go yet.

He stood beside her, slightly above her, close enough that every detail of her face, including the smudge of dirt on her chin, was visible. He had an overwhelming urge to lift his thumb and wipe it off, not because he didn't like it there but simply because he wanted an excuse to touch her face.

Her lashes were long and lowered halfway, shielding her eyes. She opened her mouth to say something but then bit down on her bottom lip.

His sights locked in on that lip, fuller than the top one. And he had the sudden image of taking that lip between his and nibbling it for himself.

She peeked up at him, almost as if she'd heard his thoughts, then immediately dropped her attention back to the rag he was holding against her burn. Were her cheeks flushing just a little? Was she feeling this attraction too?

More than just kissing her, he wanted to get to know her. Would it be too forward of him to ask if he could spend the rest of the day here with her?

Yes, it would, especially so soon after Eric's death. He'd have to give her time before he made any overtures. What would be appropriate for a grieving widow? A month?

She began to tug her hand back. "I think I'm all right."

He didn't want to release her, but holding on longer at this point would make him look desperate and maybe even deranged—if she didn't already think that about him.

He lifted the rag away but didn't move back.

She clasped both hands together in her lap. "I need to confess something, Franz."

"You do?" His heart was still racing with his desire for her. He wanted to find a scientific, logical explanation for what he was experiencing. Was it possible there was an electrical charge, even magnetic fields that existed between people? Maybe those charges—currents—grew stronger and more intense around a person with a similar current? Was it even possible certain magnetic fields meshed, as if they were meant to fit perfectly together?

She hesitated, staring down at her hands. "You should know . . ."

"Yes?" Was his voice breathless? He inwardly gave himself a mental shake. He had to stay in control of himself, or he would scare her away.

"I'm not—" She twisted at her skirt, then finally looked up at him with an apology in her green eyes.

A warning went off inside him. She was about to deliver bad news. He sucked in a breath and tried to brace himself, but a thunder of all the worst scenarios rolled through his head.

She seemed to force herself to speak. "I'm not Eric's wife."

She wasn't Eric's wife? That was all she had to say? He expelled his breath. "Thanks be to Gott."

Her brows rose.

Clearly, she hadn't been expecting his relief. But he couldn't tell her that he wanted her for himself and was glad that she didn't belong to Eric. "I was worried you were giving me bad news."

"That's not bad news?"

"It is good news." Very, very good news.

7

Clarabelle studied the man standing before her. Franz Meyer was certainly not turning out to be anything like she'd expected him to be.

Not that she'd had any expectations of him. When he'd arrived, she'd been too surprised to think beyond the simple fact that Eric's brother was here in Colorado.

Franz towered above her. He had the same light-brown hair as Eric—short, straight, and combed back. He was leaner than Eric and taller, and he had more-defined facial features that made him handsome. Not that Eric hadn't been good-looking. But Franz had a charisma and a manly appeal that likely drew women far and near.

She couldn't deny that she'd been feeling a pull toward him. It was difficult not to with how he held himself—the cock of his head, the lift of a brow, the curl of his lip—all of it directed at her as if he genuinely saw her and liked her.

And he was nice. Really nice. She'd been watching out the window when he'd started down the lane toward the house. He'd taken Dieter's capture good-naturedly. And he'd interacted with both children, not because he was obligated or because he wanted to impress anyone but because he was friendly and comfortable around children.

When she'd burned herself with coffee just a moment ago, he'd rushed to get a cold rag to put on her skin. Now he waited with the rag, as if he wanted to find another way to help her if he could.

To top it all, he'd taken the news that she wasn't Eric's wife better than she'd imagined. In fact, he didn't seem upset about the mix-up at all. He seemed relieved.

She had to clarify her role, though. He would surely want to know why she was staying with the children. Maybe once he knew that Eric had given her everything—the house, the land, his bank account, and the children—he'd be angrier. After all, Franz was a brother and uncle and deserved to have all of it more than she did.

She sat up straighter and willed herself to have the courage to tell him the whole truth about the living situation. "You're probably wondering why I'm here."

He gave a slight shrug as if to say it didn't matter to him.

But it mattered to her that she was honest with him. "Eric proposed marriage to me several days before he died."

Franz's brow furrowed, and he lowered himself to the bench beside her. "Then you did care for Eric?"

She hesitated in answering. She didn't want Franz to think she hadn't cared about Eric. Then he would surely wonder why she was there with the children. But she couldn't allow him to believe that anything had existed between her and Eric. Not when they'd been mostly just neighbors.

She hated these kinds of conversations and having to be bold and possibly make someone angry, but she forced herself to continue. "I wanted to care about your brother. I really did. He was a very kind man. But I'm sorry, I didn't have feelings for him."

"This is nothing to be sorry for." Franz reached out a hand, almost as if he intended to hold hers, but then he pulled back.

"I don't think he cared about me like that either. I truly think he just wanted me to be a mother to Dieter and Bianca."

Franz was watching her face, listening intently. "So you told him no, that you would not marry him?"

She sighed. "I tried to tell him, but I didn't do a good enough job. And so he assumed that I was willing."

"The Eric I remember could also be very persuasive when he wanted something." A twinge of bitterness edged Franz's statement. Did this have to do with the rift she'd sensed when Eric had talked about his brother not answering his letters?

"It's my fault," she persisted. "I didn't clarify my position. So he went to his solicitor and had his will made out to me."

There, she'd said everything, and now Franz would hate her.

His eyes were a dark blue, the color of the mountain peaks just after sunset. And they were wide and open and contained nothing but kindness.

"You're not upset at me?"

"Why would I be upset?"

"If you want the land and the cabin and the children, you have more of a right to them than I do. I'll go to the solicitor and have everything put in your name."

He glanced out the open doorway and watched Dieter and Bianca.

She followed his gaze to where Dieter had stopped and was holding a butterfly on a finger while showing it to Bianca. "I believe you would be a good father to them."

"They like you," he said softly.

"And I like them. But you're their family." She shifted to find that Franz was already looking at her again. "I'm just their teacher and a neighbor who's willing to help in their time of need."

"If I had not come, what would you do with them?"

She'd had a week to contemplate the future, to

consider all her alternatives. Of course, Maverick had come over every day to check on her and help her as much as he could. And she'd had the chance to talk to him about her options too. He'd still been worried about her, about her being alone with the children, and about Eric's killer still being unaccounted for.

But they'd both agreed that for now she should keep taking care of the farm as best she could. Even though she'd had more pressure from some around the community to get married and she'd even had several men mention marriage, Maverick had assured her that she shouldn't rush into anything.

So far, she and the children hadn't run into any trouble, and she'd handled all the chores just fine. In addition to the usual daily responsibilities, she'd planted the vegetable garden behind the cabin, weeded the strawberries, and even taken eggs and milk into town on two different days.

She'd also visited with Mrs. Grover, letting the kindly matron know she wouldn't be able to help at school for a while. While Clarabelle was sad about giving up her teaching dreams—at least temporarily—she knew she wouldn't have time while she was managing the farm.

She met Franz's gaze levelly, wanting him to see her honesty and sincerity. "I will always be here to help Dieter and Bianca, as long as they need me."

"You would raise them as your own?"

"I would." She would still do it if Franz was unwilling. And maybe he wouldn't want to, especially if he didn't have the financial means to take care of two children. Or maybe he had a family of his own already and couldn't be burdened.

Franz's lips curved up on one side, a dashing half smile. "I can see why Eric asked you to be their mother."

"But now that you've come, he would want you to raise them." She hadn't known Eric well, but she did know that he'd written to Franz for help before approaching her.

"I have a job I must return to in Berlin."

"Then you can take them with you. Perhaps your wife and children—"

"I am not married, nor am I in a relationship." He seemed to be watching her expectantly, as though gauging her reaction to his single status.

How could she condemn him for possibly being a single father when she was currently a single mother to the children? And Eric had been a single parent for the past year since his wife's passing. "I'm sure you could still manage them. They're good children."

"You do not think I should have a wife first?"

"Do you think I should have a husband first?"

"The influence of both a father and mother is important."

She released a tight breath. "Then you agree with

those who are pressuring me to get married?"

He stiffened, a V forming between his brows. "Pressured into marriage? What does this mean?"

"There are plenty of single men in the area who would step in to take Eric's place here." It's just that she wasn't interested in the available candidates any more than she'd been interested in Eric.

"These men should stay away from you." With a deepening scowl, he stood and folded his arms across his chest. "I do not think anyone should hurry into marriage."

"I agree."

"And you are young and should wait."

"I'm nineteen. I think that's old enough." In fact, she and Clementine would be turning twenty over the summer. "If the right man came along, I would be ready."

One of his brows quirked, softening the hard edge that had been tightening his features. "Who is the *right* man?"

"I'm not sure. Hopefully I'll know when I meet him." Was she really having this kind of conversation with a man she'd just met? She felt strangely comfortable with Franz.

Maybe the ease in relating was because he was only visiting. She'd see him for a short while, and then he'd disappear from her life.

Or maybe it was because he was such a kind person

and had a knack for putting people at ease.

A slight smile played at his lips. "Surely you must have some idea of who the right man is for you."

"I suppose so."

"Do you want him to be charming and handsome and smart, like me?" His voice held no arrogance, only teasing.

A smile of her own began to break free. "No, none of that matters."

"Really?"

"You don't believe me?"

He shrugged. "Actually, I am a confirmed bachelor and have failed quite miserably at relationships, so I cannot pretend to be the expert."

Failed? She wanted to pry, but she'd never been proficient at pressing others for personal information.

"Well?" he asked. "If not a handsome, charming, and smart man, then who?"

"I need only love."

He didn't respond, but his widening eyes reflected his disbelief.

Maybe she was being too forthright with him, but now that she'd started, she had to finish explaining herself. "I want the kind of deep and abiding love that my parents had. They were so connected that when my pa died, my ma died only months later of a broken heart." At least, that's what Clarabelle believed.

"She could not live without him?"

"Exactly."

Franz pressed a hand against his chest and fingered a necklace underneath his shirt, the outline of a chain just visible. "My parents loved each other very much also."

"I'd love to hear about them."

"And I should like to hear about yours."

Her heart warmed at the sincerity in his voice and expression, and soon she found that she was sharing about her parents, how they'd met so long ago when they'd lived in Kentucky before moving to High C Ranch and how they'd weathered many storms during their twenty-eight years of marriage.

She appreciated how well Franz listened to her and asked more questions. He was open enough to talk about his parents in return, how they'd met and fallen in love. He even shared how they'd both died.

He told her about his leaving to study at a university after their death and how he eventually become a professor. She was surprised when he asked her about her assistant teacher position and what the school was like in Breckenridge and why she hadn't gone to teacher training school yet.

One thing led to another, and soon she found that they were discussing the various methods of education and what worked best. She was especially interested to hear about his style, which involved reasoning and application rather than rote memorization.

With the passing of the morning, she invited Franz to stay for a simple lunch. Afterward, he asked her to give him a tour of the farm, and of course, Dieter and Bianca led the way, eager to show their uncle everything from the newest baby chicks to the blooms on the strawberry plants.

Franz followed along, interacting with them as if they were giving him the most interesting educational lesson known to man. Clarabelle could only watch and smile, admiring Franz all the more for his patience and sweetness with the children.

When the tour finally finished, Franz asked if they would teach him how to do some of the chores around the farm so that he might make himself useful during his visit. Although Clarabelle was curious to know what Franz meant, whether a visit would be for the day or for many days to come, she couldn't gather enough courage to ask him how long he would be in Summit County.

After they'd finished showing him how to milk the cows and feed the livestock, the afternoon had passed. Maverick had stopped by for his daily visit and met Franz. It hadn't taken Maverick long to seem at ease with the man.

As evening drew near, it seemed only natural to feed Franz supper since he'd helped with the chores. By the time they'd eaten a fare of stew and biscuits, the sun was sinking behind the western range. With darkness closing in, she convinced Franz to ride a horse back to town—one he could keep at the livery and use as long as he remained in the area.

She and the children walked down the lane with him as he led the mount. Bianca held on to one of Franz's hands and one of Clarabelle's, skipping happily between them. When they halted, Bianca and Dieter darted around trying to catch lightning bugs.

"You have already won them over." Clarabelle couldn't keep from smiling as Bianca cupped a bug and then yelped.

"They have won me also."

A beat of silence passed as they watched the children. "Eric and Luisa were good parents."

Franz's smile dimmed, as it did every time she talked about Eric and Luisa.

She waited for him to say something about the couple, about why he hadn't written back to Eric, about why he was just now coming to visit.

Instead, Franz fiddled with the lead line and ran a hand across the horse's withers. "May I come back each day and assist you and the children with the farm chores?" His question was hesitant, and his shadowed and uncertain blue eyes were the color of a mountain lake that reflected the sky.

"Of course." Was he changing his mind and deciding

to stay in Colorado and take over the place? Maybe he wanted to learn as much as he could before demanding ownership of the farm.

Whether he stayed or not, the children deserved to spend as much time getting to know their uncle as possible. "Perhaps you would consider teaching them for a short while during your stay."

He started to nod, then halted.

"Only if you want to." She hurried to put him at ease. "You probably want a break from teaching while you're away from the university."

"Not at all. I love teaching."

"It's just that I won't have time to take them into town to school, not with all the work I have to do—"

He laid a hand on her arm, silencing her. "Please, Clarabelle. I would love to teach them as much as I am able while here. And I will do it . . ." An unspoken *but* hung on the edge of his acquiescence.

"If you're too busy, I understand."

"I am not too busy." His fingers slid downward toward her wrist. With her sleeve rolled to her elbows, the touch sent a shiver of pleasure up her arm.

Surely it was just an innocent movement—one that didn't mean anything to him. And she couldn't let it mean something to her. Even so, as his fingers lingered lightly at her wrist, she found herself holding her breath and unable to look into his eyes, lest he see her reaction.

As though finally realizing he was touching her, he pulled his hand back and stuffed it into his pocket. "If time permits, would you like me to also teach you?" His question was hesitant. "It may not entirely take the place of the teacher training you aspire to, but it could be a start."

His offer was so unexpected and so generous she couldn't think of an appropriate response.

His brow was furrowed and his expression earnest. He was hatless, and strands of his hair had fallen over his forehead. With his tie pulled loose and the top button of his shirt undone, he looked almost boyish. He was more handsome now that he was slightly rumpled than he'd been earlier in the day when he'd first arrived.

Not only was he quite possibly the handsomest man she'd ever met, but he was also the kindest.

"Do not say no tonight." He fitted his hat onto his head. "At least think about it."

"I would love it." The words rushed out before she could tame her enthusiasm. "But I couldn't impose on you."

His shoulders seemed to relax, and he smiled. "I would love it also."

She smiled back, warmth cascading through her.

As he mounted and trotted down the rest of the lane, she didn't even try to hide that she was staring after him. Even as he turned onto the road, halted, and looked back, she didn't pretend to be looking elsewhere.

He didn't pretend to look anywhere else either. Not even at the children. His gaze locked on her for several long moments, making her chest tighten. He lifted his hand in a wave, then nudged his mount onward.

Only after his back was turned and he'd ridden out of sight did she expel a tense breath, one that contained a strange longing.

Oh, sweet heavens, Franz Meyer was an amazing man, and the day with him had been the best of her life.

Did that mean she was pathetic? That she needed to have more adventures and meet more people?

She wasn't sure. But one thing she was sure of—she couldn't allow her fledgling feelings to develop any further. He'd made it clear he was a confirmed bachelor and that he intended to return to Germany to his university teaching position. If he didn't want to make room in his life for the children, then he wouldn't make room in his life for a wife either.

Yes, the best thing to do was to see Franz as a loving uncle to Dieter and Bianca and not make more of an attraction than necessary.

Now if only she could convince her heart to follow the advice.

8

Who would want to murder Eric?

Franz stepped out the front door and past the sign that read, *Addison M. Irving, Esq. Attorney at Law. Wills, Deeds filled, Disputes settled, Notary, Bondsman, Patents reviewed.*

Franz had been at the office upon its opening at nine o'clock sharp. Mr. Irving had been welcoming and had also expressed all the right condolences for the loss of a brother. The lawyer had read Eric's will, and it was just as Clarabelle had indicated. Not that Franz had doubted her. Not at all. She'd proven herself to be true and loyal yesterday within a short time of meeting her.

But he had hoped his visit with Mr. Irving would provide some clarification for why anyone would want to murder Eric, who'd clearly kept his familial identity a secret and was known only as a poor German immigrant farmer.

As far as anyone in the community knew, Eric had nothing of value, nothing to steal, nothing to claim, nothing to entice anyone. Certainly, no one would covet his fields or his tiny home. Not when land was nearly free in the West under the Homestead Act.

Of course, Eric had purchased his land outright, having taken a meager amount of gold and silver with him when he'd left Germany. Franz had insisted on Eric having all that rightfully belonged to him, but Eric had said he hadn't wanted anything but forgiveness.

At the time, Franz had been too hurt, angry, and bitter to consider forgiving Eric, even after his brother had renounced his claim on the estate as firstborn and had given everything to Franz except the small amount that would help him get a fresh start in a new land.

Franz had scoffed at the inheritance, had believed Eric was using it to appease him—or perhaps even buy the forgiveness he'd sought. So instead of claiming the bulk of the inheritance and living at the estate on Lake Tollensesee, Franz had closed up the castle and moved to Berlin. A small number of loyal staff still maintained the home and grounds, but Franz had only gone back a couple of times over the years.

As a nobleman, the son of a baron, he hadn't needed to work for a living. Regardless, he'd spent every waking moment devoting himself to becoming a world-renowned professor, staying too busy to think much about Eric and Luisa.

Now, after years of arduous work, he'd proven that he hadn't gotten the job because of his title and wealth and his family's connection to the emperor. He'd earned it through diligence and determination like any common man.

Franz stepped onto the boardwalk, which was partly caked with dried mud. The air was cool for a June morning, but it was light and invigorating and clean. He took a deep breath, letting it clear away the nagging headache that had plagued him the past couple of nights, likely part of the altitude adjustment that everyone in Denver had warned him about.

After all, Breckenridge stood at 9,600 feet of elevation compared to the 5,000 of Denver. Berlin was a measly 115 feet above sea level. Here, he was practically on top of the world, or at least, it felt that way. Of course, he'd studied enough geography to know that the Rocky Mountains weren't nearly the tallest peaks in the world. All the same, now that he was here, he was glad he'd made the trip.

He peered past the weathered false fronts of the businesses lining Main Street to the rising mountains behind the town. They were rockier and more barren than he'd expected above the tree line, the alpine tundra zone with low-growing grasses and shrubs.

Sometime before he left, he'd have to hire a guide to take him on a hiking expedition into the higher peaks.

Surely such an adventure would provide plenty of interesting information to share with his students when he returned home.

He shifted his gaze to the road running north following the Blue River as it led to Eric's farm and to Clarabelle and the children. From the moment he'd awoken this morning, he'd been eager to ride back out and see them again. He'd actually done little else but think about Clarabelle since leaving her last evening.

Yes, he was worried that she was living alone in the wilderness with two little children. What woman did that? Especially with an unsolved murder that had recently taken place. Even though she wore a pistol, how would she fend for herself and the children if the murderer really did return?

More than worrying about her, he simply admired everything about her, from her beauty to her tender spirit to her sacrificial attitude with the children. She'd been easy to talk to and companionable and even fun. He'd enjoyed spending the day with her and the children, watching them at work, listening to their tales of adventure, and getting to know them.

And he wanted to find a way to help them, make their lives easier . . . at least in the short term. Maybe he'd even find a way to transfer a portion of the inheritance over to the children so that they wouldn't ever be in need.

In the meantime, he needed to find out more about

Eric during the last months of his life and try to discover whom—if anyone—Eric had offended or made enemies with. It was difficult to imagine Eric offending or making an enemy of anyone, but maybe his brother had changed over the years of living in America and had intermingled with the wrong type of people.

Franz turned his steps down the boardwalk toward the store he'd passed last evening on his way into town. The bright lights that had emanated from within the store had illuminated a shelf of books. He hoped that among them he'd find some children's books that he could use in teaching Bianca and Dieter their lessons. Maybe there would even be a book that would be helpful in teaching Clarabelle. He would also check if the store sold slates and chalk. Even paper and pencils would do.

He'd brought along only a couple of his favorite volumes, both in German. And although he didn't necessarily need any books to teach, it would make the lessons easier.

The name *Worth's General Store* was painted in bold, black letters on the false front above the door. The big front window was spotless, showing a display of sturdy boots, leather gloves, and a matching leather coat.

As he peered past the items, his gaze snagged upon a woman with blond-red hair in a long braid down her back. Although the woman was facing away from the window, there was no mistaking Clarabelle. From the elegant line of her neck to the slender waist to the long legs hidden beneath her skirt, her body was as beautiful and perfect today as it had been yesterday.

The image of her face was at the front of his mind— the sweetness of her smile, the bright green of her eyes, and the gentleness in every curve of her chin and cheeks.

His gut tightened with that same need that had been building since meeting her—a need that still defied rational explanation, that burned through him and couldn't be extinguished. Not that he'd tried to extinguish it. In fact, with all his thinking about her over the night, he'd probably only made the flames inside hotter.

She was standing in front of one of the counters, opening the glass containers on the top—jars of various sizes filled with an assortment of colorful candy.

With the heat swelling in his gut, he opened the door and stepped into the store, the tinkle of a bell as well as the scent of cinnamon and sugar welcoming him. Several customers were milling about the floor-to-ceiling shelves that lined the walls as well as a double-sided set of shelves at the center of the store.

A middle-aged man wearing an apron stood at the rear of the store, conversing with one of the patrons. He nodded a friendly greeting to Franz but didn't cease his discussion.

That was all right with Franz. The purchase of books

could wait. All he wanted to do at the moment was see Clarabelle and talk with her. Maybe he would even suggest accompanying her back to the farm when she was done with her shopping.

He wasted no time in approaching her, and a part of him wished he'd thought to pick her a bouquet of wildflowers from the smattering of flowers he'd noticed behind the hotel this morning when he'd looked out his window.

Instead, he quieted his tread. As soon as he was behind her, he snaked his hands around her head, covered her eyes, and leaned in. "Guess who?" He was so happy to see her he didn't care that his voice reflected his pleasure and was slightly breathy.

Clarabelle stiffened, and her hands on the jars froze.

He couldn't hold back his grin.

"Should I know you?" she asked with a curious ring to her voice.

"Yes." She hadn't forgotten about him overnight, had she?

"Hmm . . ." Her voice turned playful. "I don't know. Are you a secret admirer?"

"Do you want me to be?"

"Of course. I'd never turn away a secret admirer, especially one who smells as good as you do." She sniffed at his coat sleeve.

He almost cringed at her strange observation and

behavior, but he held himself back. He had put on an extra pat of aftershave this morning after completing his grooming. Maybe the scent still lingered on his hands.

"You look enchanting this morning." He dropped his hands away and took a step back.

"I do?"

"Very."

She released the candy jars and turned to face him. The magnetic energy that had charged the air yesterday between himself and Clarabelle was gone. Not even the tiniest electron was sparking.

Strange disappointment wafted through him. He should have known she'd been too good to be true and that what he'd felt with her was too powerful to be real. As pretty as she still was, the spell that had held him captive yesterday had broken.

He ought to be relieved. The very idea of loving her so quickly had been difficult to believe anyway.

She was sweeping her gaze over him much more boldly than she had before, her eyes holding frank appreciation. "You look enchanting, too, Mr. . . .?"

Obviously she had forgotten about him. "Mr. Meyer? Franz?"

As she propped a hand on one of her hips, she lifted her shoulders, as if she was conscious of how beautiful and womanly she was and was waiting for him to notice her again.

But today, he wasn't interested in looking at her. His lust was locked away where it belonged.

As her lips curved up into what he could only describe as a seductive smile, he noticed a smattering of freckles on her nose that hadn't been there yesterday as well as a scar on her chin. And her skin. It wasn't as pale but was instead a tanner complexion.

What had happened?

The bell above the door jangled again and another man stepped inside—a stocky cowboy in a flannel shirt, denim trousers, and tall boots. Underneath a Stetson he had dark-brown hair and shadowed dark eyes. He was the same fellow who had been working at the livery last night when Franz had asked for a stall to rent.

The man's attention rode straight to Clarabelle, as if he'd laid a claim on her long ago and had no intention of letting any other man encroach.

Clarabelle had mentioned that other men would marry her if she'd let them. Was this one of the candidates?

"I wouldn't buy what she's selling, if I were you." The man was speaking to Franz but had his eyes narrowed upon Clarabelle. "Last time Clementine offered me a piece of her candy, she tried to kill me with it."

Clementine?

Franz's gaze flipped back to the young woman. And this time he noticed even more changes from yesterday—

looser and messier hair, the firmer press of her lips, a sassier lift of her chin.

"Don't worry, Grady." The young woman glared back at the newcomer. "The only one I want to keel over is you."

This wasn't Clarabelle. Who was she?

"You can't get rid of me that easily." The young man gave a curt shake of his head before stomping toward the rear of the establishment.

The store owner, presumably Mr. Worth, had halted his conversation and was watching the two interact with a raised brow, as if he was accustomed to such bickering and found it more amusing than irritating.

"Sorry for bothering you, Dad," the young man said as he approached the store owner. "But I got taken with counterfeit bills again. Some fellow this morning paid up, and I didn't realize the money was fake until he was long gone."

The woman—Clementine—was still glaring at Grady.

The distraction gave Franz a moment to try to collect himself and his thoughts. Was it possible Clarabelle had a twin sister? She hadn't mentioned anything about it, but that would be the natural conclusion, and the only thing left to do was ask.

He cleared his throat, hoping to garner the woman's attention.

She seemed to tear her gaze from the livery owner or manager or whatever his position was. As she did so, she forced a bright smile. "Now, where were we before we were so rudely interrupted?"

In the middle of speaking to the store owner, Grady snorted, clearly still paying attention to Clementine even though he was making an attempt not to.

Clementine stepped toward Franz, took hold of both of his coat lapels. "I think you were telling me how enchanting I looked today and that you wanted to be my secret admirer."

She was likely putting on a show for Grady, and Franz didn't have the heart to let her know he'd mistaken her for Clarabelle. He wouldn't embarrass her like that so publicly. It wouldn't hurt anything to play along with her for a moment and then later confess to his mix-up.

"You do look very enchanting." He held his ground and didn't draw nearer to her, even though she seemed to be trying to pull him even closer.

She smiled up at him, and in that smile he caught a glimpse of Clarabelle that made his heart flip. "You're very kind. And *gentlemanly*." She emphasized the word as she slanted another look at Grady. "Unlike some of the men in this town."

"I do try to be a gentleman." Franz actually wouldn't know how to behave in an uncouth manner, even if he tried. He'd been born and bred to be a nobleman, a leader, and a gentleman in every sense of the word.

Clementine was studying his face more intently now. "Because you are such a gentleman and so handsome, I invite you to come calling on me . . . uh . . . Franz."

At the rear of the store, Grady paused for several heartbeats.

Her gaze slid to the young man as though she was gauging his reaction. Just as quickly, her attention came to rest on Franz, her green eyes wide, her expression hopeful.

All the customers in the store had stopped and were watching her.

Franz sighed inwardly. He couldn't very well turn her down now. He'd have to continue the pretense and then correct her later. He sensed she wouldn't be too heartbroken. Not when she seemed to crave Grady's attention more than anything else.

Franz gave a polite bow. "I would be honored to call upon you."

"Friday evening for supper?"

"Of course."

"I live on High C Ranch, north of town. Follow the road along the river for about two miles, and you'll eventually reach our place. There's a sign above the gate you can't miss."

Yes, this woman was most definitely Clarabelle's sister.

He politely extricated himself from the store and managed to reclaim his horse at the livery before Grady returned. Franz was relieved when he was finally on his way to see Clarabelle and the children. He hadn't bothered to stay and purchase the books—would save that for another day when neither Clementine nor Grady was in the store.

As he reached the lane and turned down it toward the cabin, his heart pounded with a rush of anticipation. After the interaction with Clementine, he wasn't sure what to expect with Clarabelle. What if he'd only just imagined the attraction yesterday? Even if it had been there, what if it were gone now?

He could see Clarabelle and the children at the far side of the strawberry field, busy at work pulling weeds.

Bianca was the first to notice him. She pushed up and waved both arms, jumping up and down. Dieter stood next, and Clarabelle sat back on her heels, pausing in her work as she watched his approach.

Today she had on a wide straw hat that tied under her chin with a blue ribbon. She wore a simple blue skirt and blouse, but even from a distance, she radiated beauty and gentleness and peace—so much so that the worry pinging through his head seemed to fade into silence.

He rode his horse past the house and the barn, too eager to be near her to stop. Upon reaching the edge of the field, he slid down from his mount. The children had already wound through the plants to meet him. Clarabelle was standing and watching them, as though uncertain what kind of greeting would be appropriate.

He interacted for several moments with the children, crouching in front of them, listening to their tales of how they'd awoken to find a fox stalking the chicken coop and how Clarabelle had fired a shot into the air to scare it away.

When he couldn't bear the distance from her a second longer, he rose and started across the field toward her. With one of the children's hands in each of his own, they stepped carefully so as not to disturb the plants.

"Good morning," he said to her when he was only a dozen paces away.

She tilted up the wide brim of her hat to reveal her innocent eyes. Eyes that were filled with quiet patience and steady loyalty and gracious welcome.

And beauty . . .

His pulse picked up its pace and began to race as fast as a thoroughbred on the last course. She was stunning with the morning sunlight cascading over her, turning her hair to golden fire and her eyes to a lush green that rivaled the thick fields.

Even though she looked nearly identical to Clementine, he wasn't sure how he'd mistaken her. There was no comparison. Clarabelle was in a world of her own, where no one or nothing could begin to equal her.

"Good morning." She offered him a shy smile, as if she'd heard his thoughts. Or perhaps she'd seen the attraction flaring in his eyes.

"I met your twin this morning."

"You did?"

"From behind I thought she was you."

"When we were little, we used to fool even our parents."

"As soon as she turned, I recognized the differences nearly right away."

"It's easier to tell us apart now that we're adults." Clarabelle lifted a hand to her face to wipe at her cheek. Her fingers were soiled and left a streak behind.

Gott in heaven, have mercy upon his poor soul. She was so beautiful at this moment, standing among the flowering strawberry plants, even with her smudges.

He needn't have worried about having only imagined his reaction to her. Everything he'd been feeling for her yesterday was sparking with even more energy. The magnetic field between them was indeed very real and strong. It was pulling him toward her with a power that he seemed helpless to resist—not that he wanted to resist her.

He was already hopelessly and helplessly captivated by this woman.

9

She'd never met a man like Franz Meyer.

With the darkness of evening settling in, he'd left for town. Clarabelle stood with the children halfway down the lane, where they'd walked with him before he'd mounted and started on his way.

She'd thought the previous day had been wonderful, but today had been even more perfect. From the moment Franz had arrived, everything had seemed to fall into place with the world, as if she hadn't truly been awake and alive until he'd crossed the strawberry field and told her good morning.

He'd knelt among the plants and helped with the weeding. When they'd finished, they'd gone into the cabin, and she'd made a fresh pot of coffee and kept him supplied while he'd instructed the children with methods she'd never witnessed before, using manipulatives and demonstrations, even taking them outside and using real life illustrations.

She'd learned so much just watching him. He'd stirred her curiosity and sense of wonder, and she'd wanted to keep going, to learn even more, but their rumbling stomachs had forced them to stop for lunch.

Much to her surprise, he'd asked if they wanted to take their lunch outside and have a picnic. Then together, they'd tended to the chores they'd neglected during the morning. She'd still had some of the garden to finish planting, and he'd headed into the barn with the children to muck stalls and fill the watering troughs.

He'd stayed for supper again, and when they'd finished, he'd acted out an old fairy tale: "Little Red Riding Hood" by the Brothers Grimm. He'd had the children participate with him, helping them get into their characters, showing them how to change their voices and speak their lines, all the while fostering creativity.

Bianca slipped her hand into Clarabelle's as they watched Franz ride away. "I like Uncle Franz." The little girl was still attired in a red blanket they'd found in one of the trunks and utilized for her role of Red Riding Hood.

"I like him too." Dieter was wearing a dark cloak and carrying a blunt axe as the woodsman.

Clarabelle had to swallow hard to keep from saying anything. Because she was sure if she opened her mouth to add that she liked Franz, her declaration would be much too ardent.

As Franz turned onto the main road, he slowed his mount and shifted in his saddle as he'd done last night. Across the distance and past the trees, he was still visible, the last rays of the setting sun gleaming on him.

He sought them out and raised his hand in a final wave. And he was looking directly at her again.

Her heart fluttered with a longing for him that had been building throughout the day. It was a longing she didn't quite understand—one she'd never experienced before.

She lifted a hand and waved back, satisfied in a way she hadn't felt in a long time, maybe since before Pa and Ma had died.

What was it about Franz Meyer that made her so happy?

She couldn't keep from smiling at him as he lingered, looking back at her. Almost as if he couldn't tear himself away. Which wasn't true, was it?

Bianca slipped her hand into Clarabelle's. "Do you like Uncle Franz?"

Clarabelle squeezed the little girl's hand. "Of course I do. He's a very nice man."

"Maybe you can marry him."

Marry Franz? Clarabelle's pulse hopped erratically at just the thought—a completely new reaction to marriage, the first of its kind ever. That had to mean something, didn't it? That what she was feeling for Franz had the potential to become more?

"Then you can still become our mother." Dieter's voice filled with excitement. "And Uncle Franz can be our father."

The children missed their father terribly. The past week had been difficult for them without him, especially at night. Not only did Bianca have a difficult time going to sleep, but she woke up almost every night crying.

Clarabelle knew the children didn't want to replace their father, but she guessed they were worried about what would happen and wanted a normal life—or as normal as possible after losing both parents.

Was having Franz stay the answer to all the problems?

Even as Clarabelle's thoughts began to spiral like they were caught in a gust of wind, she sucked in a breath and shut off the air flow to the idea of having more with Franz. "I'm sorry, children. But your Uncle Franz intends to return to Germany."

Dieter lifted expectant eyes to her. "Maybe if he falls in love with you, he'll want to stay here."

"He has an important job there as a professor at a big university."

"Then we'll go with him," Bianca said as if the answer were really that simple.

Franz had already indicated that his life was full enough without the children, much less a wife. "I'm afraid Uncle Franz isn't the type of man who wants to get married. At twenty-eight, if he'd wanted to get married, I think he already would have."

The children were silent at her declaration, both of their foreheads furrowed in thought.

Franz had only ridden a dozen paces when a horse and rider traveling north approached him. From the sunlight slanting upon the new rider, Clarabelle recognized her right away. Clementine. Her twin sister was coming home from town. Lately she'd been spending longer days at the general store, helping Mr. Worth with customers as well as selling her candy.

Of course, she still had to make the candy and spent at least two days a week in the ranch kitchen creating her increasingly popular sweets. Clarabelle had often helped, doing anything Clementine needed from her—stirring bubbling pots of syrup, dipping candy into melted chocolate, pouring molds of colorful creations, washing pots and pans and mixing bowls.

Now, as Clementine halted next to Franz, something sharp pinched Clarabelle's chest. What was Clementine doing talking with Franz? Surely it was nothing more than a friendly greeting. Because earlier, when Franz had mentioned meeting Clementine, he hadn't seemed enamored or infatuated the way most men were.

Clarabelle's muscles tensed as Clementine let her head fall back in a laugh in response to something Franz said.

Given Franz's angle, she couldn't see his reaction, but if he were behaving like every other man in Summit County, then he was probably grinning and nodding and agreeing to do whatever Clementine suggested.

Because that's how Clementine was. She was flirtatious even when she didn't realize it, and Franz would have no power to resist her. Not if she laid on her full charm. No man could resist her.

Clarabelle had only to think back on all the boys and young men who'd come and gone from their lives during the fourteen years their family had lived in Colorado. Without fail, everyone had fallen for Clementine first, hadn't even really seen Clarabelle standing in her sister's shadow.

Clarabelle shifted into a patch of fading sunlight. This time was different, wasn't it? Franz was hers. She'd been the one to meet him first, and Clementine had no right to have him.

With a nod, Franz nudged his horse onward. Clementine watched him for several heartbeats, as though waiting for him to turn around and look at her again. Thankfully, he didn't and kept going without a backward glance.

Clarabelle eased the tension from her shoulders, relieved he hadn't lingered with Clementine the same way that he had with her and the children.

As soon as she felt the relief, she silently rebuked

herself. Hadn't she just admonished the children that nothing could happen with her and Franz, that he had no interest in a wife—her or any other woman?

He most certainly wasn't *hers*.

As Clementine started forward again, she caught sight of Clarabelle and the children and waved with an excited shout. A minute later, Clementine had dismounted, given Bianca and Dieter hugs as well as a piece each of hard candy, and was ambling slowly toward the cabin alongside Clarabelle.

"So, Franz is quite the dreamy fellow, isn't he?" Clementine released a sigh that sent needles pricking along Clarabelle's spine. She'd heard that sigh before and knew exactly what it meant—that Clementine was already enamored.

Clarabelle didn't want her twin to think Franz was dreamy or anything else. Did he have any negative characteristics? Anything at all to turn Clementine against him? "He's a very practical man. Studious. Serious. And old . . . he's twenty-eight."

Clementine peered up at the dusk sky, a soft smile curving her lips—one that said none of the negative traits had dissuaded her from liking Franz. "He's so handsome."

Clarabelle shrugged as if she hadn't noticed exactly how handsome Franz was. But of course, she'd done nothing but notice his striking features all day. Every time

WILLING TO WED THE RANCHER

he'd smiled or laughed, she'd wanted to stop time and simply stare at him, but she'd done her best to act as normal as possible so that she didn't send him running back to Germany to get away from her.

Clementine released another happy sigh. "His blue eyes are so beautiful and piercing."

"He wears spectacles when he reads."

"I'm sure they make him look distinguished."

"Or stuffy."

Clementine laughed lightly. "That man is anything but stuffy. There's something about him that just oozes manliness."

Her sister was absolutely right, but Clarabelle couldn't say so. "He isn't planning to stay here. He's going back to Germany."

"I'd go with him anywhere."

"And be uprooted from everyone you love and everything you know?"

"Think of all the adventures I'd have."

Clarabelle halted, frustration mounting with each of her sister's comments. Clearly, Clementine liked Franz, and none of the negative comments were changing her mind.

"He's not the type of man you can trifle with, Clem. Not like all the other men."

Clementine stopped too. "I realize that. It's one of the things that appeals to me. He's different."

Franz *was* different. Clarabelle had already established that. But why did Clementine have to see that too? And why did she have to be attracted to him?

Clarabelle scrambled to find any other way to discourage her sister and landed on the best excuse of all. "He told me he's a confirmed bachelor, so you should put him from your mind, or you'll only get hurt."

Clementine's smile turned smug. "He's calling on me Friday night."

Clarabelle's heart dropped to the bottom of her chest. Franz was calling on Clementine? Really?

Of course he was. Why wouldn't he be more interested in Clementine than he was in her? It was bound to happen. Even though Clarabelle had felt something with him that she'd never felt with anyone else, apparently he hadn't felt the same in return, or at least in the same measure.

Under the canopy of aspens in the growing darkness of the evening, the soft stuttering trill of toads wafted in the air along with the laughter of the children as they raced ahead.

"Hold on, now." Clementine's smile disappeared and concern filled her eyes. "You don't mind that he's calling on me, do you?"

Clementine must have noticed or sensed the dismay.

Clarabelle swallowed hard. How could she tell her sister that, yes, she really did mind, that she didn't want to give up Franz? She couldn't, not when Franz wasn't hers to begin with. "He's welcome to call on anyone he wants to."

Clementine studied her face. "After the way you were just talking about him, I didn't think you liked him."

Had her strategy of listing all his negative qualities worked to her disadvantage? How could she possibly admit that she hadn't wanted Clementine to like him? "He does have some nice qualities too."

"Listen, honey." Clementine swept a messy strand of hair behind her ear. "If you like Franz even a little, I'll let him know that I don't want him calling on me. I'll cancel the dinner plans."

If Franz had asked to call on Clementine, then what good would it do to stop him? He was obviously intrigued and attracted by Clementine enough to pursue her, enough to make plans to visit with her.

Clarabelle tried not to shiver as the cool evening breeze swept under her skirt and blouse. How could she interfere with what Franz wanted? And why would she want to? Not when he hadn't been intrigued or attracted enough to pursue her instead.

Besides, she couldn't deny Clementine anything. She never had been able to.

She gave her sister a smile—one she hoped was genuine and filled with love. "You know I just want you to be happy. And if Franz will make you happy, then I want you to see him." Her statement was mostly true. She did want Clementine to be happy. But why did it have to be with Franz?

"You're sure?" Clementine was still watching her carefully. "You seem hesitant."

The children's voices rose near the cabin. Bianca stuck out her tongue at Dieter, and he crossed his arms and glared back. While the two interacted well together most of the time, the bickering was more frequent than Clarabelle preferred. Would Clementine manage them better?

"If you start seeing Franz, you'll have to get to know the children too, won't you?"

Clementine nodded, gazing at Bianca and Dieter and then back at her. "Oh, so that's it. You like living here and taking care of the children and don't want to lose this?"

Was that part of the hesitation too? "I'm sure everything will work out the way it's supposed to."

"You do know that someday you'll find a man who loves you and will give you a family of your own, don't you?" Clementine's tone held a note of pity.

Irritation rose swiftly inside Clarabelle. She never liked when Clementine felt sorry for her that she didn't get attention from young men. It always made her feel worse.

"I'll be fine," she said, forcing another smile. "And if

you end up loving Franz and the children, they'd be very blessed to have you in their lives."

Clementine hesitated only a moment more before her smile came out in full bloom and the dreamy look with it. "If he proposed tomorrow, I'd accept. I'm ready to move from the ranch and start my own life."

Something in her sister's voice halted Clarabelle's irritation. She knew Clementine was exaggerating, that she wouldn't really accept a proposal tomorrow. But clearly, her sister was having a harder time living on the ranch than she'd let on. Maybe she felt out of place being there with Maverick and Hazel as newlyweds. Maybe she missed Clarabelle's presence. Or maybe it was difficult being there with all the memories of Ma everywhere.

Whatever the case, Clarabelle knew what she had to do. She had to step out of the way so that she didn't deter Franz in any way from pursuing Clementine, especially if courting Franz would make Clementine happy again and help her through the grief of losing Ma.

10

"So no one found the murder weapon?" Franz stood with the sheriff near the barn.

"Reckon whoever done it got rid of all the evidence." The sheriff chewed on a long piece of grass, leaning casually against the wood pile Franz had slowly been adding to whenever he had a chance, like this morning.

Except for the star pinned to his vest, the sheriff looked like any other average fellow in the area. His gaze was riveted to Clarabelle where she was hanging garments on a clothesline near the cabin. The wind had picked up and was not only flapping at the damp linens but molding Clarabelle's blouse and skirt to her body, showing off all her curves.

Franz cleared his throat, trying to draw the sheriff's attention away from Clarabelle, but the fellow didn't take the hint to keep his eyes off what didn't belong to him.

Franz had the sudden urge to go over to Clarabelle

and offer to finish hanging the clothing for her. But the truth was, Clarabelle didn't belong to him either.

If only the sheriff wasn't looking at Clarabelle like he was removing every article of her clothing and hanging them right on the line with the damp items. It was disrespectful.

Besides, the man had to be in his thirties, if not early forties. Even if he was single, he was too old for a woman as young and innocent as Clarabelle. Not that Franz considered himself young. But he prided himself on having some decency. When he felt himself starting to lust over Clarabelle, he made a concerted effort to stop and change the direction of his thoughts.

It hadn't been easy during the past week of being around her for the better part of each day. All too often he found himself admiring her beauty and longing for her. In fact, he constantly felt the pull to be close to her, even just to stand near her. He loved watching her interactions with the children. He loved seeing the contentment on her face whenever she finished a task. He loved listening to her laughter. He loved the way her eyes lit up when they had deeper discussions.

Each night, he was having a more difficult time tearing himself away from her. And when he was back at his hotel room, the desire to be with her again was so keen that his sleep was becoming restless.

And he'd only been in Breckenridge for about a week.

If he already felt this way about her after a week, how would he feel after two weeks or a month?

Maybe he needed to cut short his stay before the bond with her was so strong that he wouldn't want to leave. Because he had to return to the university and all that he was accomplishing with his innovative teaching methods. He was making a difference, changing minds, creating independent thinkers. Besides, he'd never be satisfied with being a simple farmer here. Sure, he was enjoying getting to experience what farm life was like, but he didn't want to do it indefinitely.

Of course, he'd considered what life would be like if Clarabelle and the children came back with him. What would she think about moving to a strange land where she would be far from her family and wouldn't be able to speak the language? They'd have to reside in Berlin for portions of the year, and after living in this wide-open wilderness, how would she and the children ever be able to adjust?

Behind him in the barn, he could hear Bianca's giggles. She and Dieter were supposed to be laying fresh hay in the cow stalls, but Franz had glimpsed them building a hay pile and jumping into it. He hadn't the heart to reprimand them. Not when they were finding joy in such simple things.

It wouldn't be fair to ask them to give up everything for him. In fact, he felt rather ludicrous even contemplating the possibility of being with Clarabelle, since he'd just met her. He might be experiencing this powerful attraction to her, but she hadn't been as enthusiastic with him.

She was sweet and kind and friendly, but it felt like she'd already decided that she would view him only as the children's uncle and nothing more. She hadn't said or done anything to make him feel unwelcome or unlikeable, but a barrier was there nonetheless.

The sheriff spat out the piece of grass and pushed away from the wood pile. "We've done about all we can to solve this here murder, and now it's time to just let things go." Was there an edge of warning in the sheriff's tone?

Franz rubbed a sleeve across the perspiration forming on his forehead and pretended not to notice the threat. He wasn't about to let things go. Not today, not tomorrow—not until he discovered the truth. But rather than being too direct or antagonistic, he had to be as amiable as possible if he had any hope of getting further in his investigation.

So far, everyone he'd questioned had been forthcoming in sharing all they knew about Eric and his activities. From everything Franz had learned, Eric had lived a quiet and secluded life, but he'd also been well respected in the community for his work ethic, generosity, and kindness. That meant the murder hadn't been a result of neighborly disputes or grudges from townspeople.

He'd also decided the murder wasn't related to an angry customer. From what he'd gathered, Eric had a stellar business reputation. He'd always offered fair prices and trades on his goods, had never tried cheating anyone, and had conducted his transactions above reproach.

"Heard tell you're only here for a visit, that you ain't staying." The sheriff straightened his hat, still openly gawking at Clarabelle.

"I would like to make sure my nephew and niece and Clarabelle are well situated before I return home."

"Reckon that oughta be soon." The sheriff rested a hand on his pistol.

So that's why the sheriff had ridden out to the farm today. Not to answer any questions Franz had about the murder. No, from how tight-lipped the sheriff had been during their brief discussion, that had just been an excuse—an excuse to warn him to stop investigating the crime and go home where he belonged.

Franz picked up the axe that he'd rested against the woodpile. His fingers and the blisters on his palm started aching just thinking about chopping more wood. Even though he was still fumbling through most of the farm tasks, he was still appreciating the experience of the manual labor and the lessons he was learning.

"Thank you for your visit today." Franz nodded at the

man. Even if the sheriff hadn't disclosed a single clue, at least Franz could now conclude something bigger was going on in the area—something the sheriff knew about and was protecting. Whatever that was, somehow Eric had gotten drawn in, perhaps inadvertently. That had likely been the danger he'd mentioned in his letter, and that danger had ultimately cost him his life.

Franz righted the half-chopped log that had toppled over. He'd also concluded that he needed to move forward with the investigation more cautiously. If he wasn't careful, he'd not only endanger himself but also Clarabelle and the children. And he didn't want to do that.

The sheriff took a step toward his horse, then paused. "You should know that people are starting to yammer on about you and Clarabelle being here alone all the time. Ain't good for her reputation."

"I appreciate knowing that, Sheriff." The last thing Franz wanted to do was harm her good name and character in the community.

"All the more reason for you to be taking your leave. That way another fella can marry her proper-like."

"I will ponder your advice." Franz kept his tone as friendly as possible, even as his insides roiled with frustration.

As the sheriff rode away, the frustration only swirled with more intensity. He hadn't considered how his presence on his brother's farm would affect Clarabelle's reputation. Was he doing her more harm than good by coming out and helping?

As she finished hanging the clothing to dry, his gaze strayed to her more times than he wanted to admit. She finally gathered the laundry tin and washboard and soap and headed his way. To store the supplies in the barn. Not to visit with him.

Even though he wished she'd show more interest in him, he admired her for not being like other women who encouraged his attention—like her sister, Clementine. He'd encountered her a couple of times over the past few days, and each time, she'd been flirtatious, making an obvious attempt to engage him.

He should have canceled the plans to call on her. But he'd forgotten about the invitation until just that morning before he'd ridden out of town when she'd reminded him that she was looking forward to their dinner tonight.

Even then, he'd been tempted to tell her he had to cancel. But he was too much of a gentleman to be so rude and had decided that at some point during the evening, he'd clarify he wasn't interested in pursuing a relationship with her. He never should have agreed to the dinner and couldn't even remember why he'd felt the need to say yes.

"Is it time for the children's lessons?" He let the axe fall idle and tugged at his shirt collar, pulling it away from his sticky neck. The June day was proving to be the warmest yet, which, according to Clarabelle, would be good for the strawberries and newly planted garden.

Clarabelle paused beside him, her eyes twinkling with humor as she peered through the open barn doors to where the children were playing instead of working. "It sounds like they're having fun."

"They are indeed." Did Clarabelle ever take the time to have fun? She was always working hard at one task or another when he was at the farm. Even when he was giving the children their lessons, she was busy baking or cooking or cleaning up after a meal or doing some other household chore.

Even though she'd agreed to let him teach her, she hadn't yet taken the time to sit down with him when he'd offered. She always had one excuse or another. It wasn't because she didn't want to learn. She listened while he was teaching the children, and he could see that she thoroughly enjoyed all his demonstrations and illustrations and reenactments.

No, her reticence had more to do with him. Maybe she was hesitant to spend time alone with him.

As she fumbled to hold the laundering supplies, he set his axe down and reached for the tub and scrubbing board, relieving her of the burden.

She offered him a grateful smile—one that made her face even prettier. "Thank you, Franz. Your help has been such a blessing this week."

"I wish I could do more." Like employ several people to work the farm so that she didn't have to do so much. He'd considered the option for after he returned to Germany, but he always came to the conclusion that he'd have to hire men, since women were in such short supply in the mountains. And hiring men was out of the question. Not when most seemed to want wives.

"You're already doing more than is necessary." She continued through the barn door, and he followed.

At the sight of them, the children raced to pick up their discarded shovels. She gently scolded them, letting them know that as a result of their negligence, their lessons would now be delayed.

They set right to work diligently, eager for their school time. And once they finished a short while later, Franz helped them hang their tools on the barn wall. Clarabelle was outside in the paddock with the horses, checking their shoes.

She was exceptionally good with horses, likely because she'd grown up around them on her family's horse ranch.

"You like Clarabelle, don't you, Uncle Franz?" Dieter stood beside him, staring out the barn door at Clarabelle too. Bianca was next to Dieter, feet spread and arms crossed the same way as her brother.

Franz glanced down at his own spread feet and crossed arms. Both children were imitating him.

He took a rapid step back into the barn before Clarabelle glanced their way and saw all three of them watching her like lunatics. Because that's what he was turning into. A lunatic.

Even Dieter had noticed his attraction and had followed him into the shadows of the barn, watching him expectantly, waiting for an answer to his question.

He couldn't admit the strength of his feelings for Clarabelle to the children. It wouldn't be appropriate in the least. But he also couldn't lie.

"It's okay if you want to marry her, Uncle Franz." Bianca was peering up at him with her petite face that never failed to remind him of Luisa. Even though seeing Luisa in her had been difficult at first, he'd realized it wasn't Bianca's fault and that she deserved his very best in spite of everything that had happened.

He'd hoped to use the journey to America to repair his relationship with Eric, but since he was too late for that, perhaps the journey was more about releasing the past and learning to let go of all the hurt.

"We already talked with Clarabelle about marrying you." Dieter spoke the words solemnly. "And she said she would."

"She did?" He couldn't keep his gaze from finding her again, taking her in much too eagerly.

Dieter hesitated. "She said you wouldn't want to marry her because you have an important job and because you're twenty-eight."

A spurt of indignation shot through him. "What does my age have to do with it?"

Dieter shrugged. "You don't look too old to me, Uncle Franz."

"That is because I am not too old." He braced his shoulders, but as soon as he did, an ache in his lower back from chopping wood nearly buckled him over as if to taunt him that his youth was fading.

Maybe it was time to prove to Clarabelle, and even to himself, that he was still young enough to do anything he set his mind to.

He pressed a finger to his lips, the usual stance he took whenever he needed to think. Hadn't he just been lamenting that Clarabelle worked too much? Perhaps it was time to insist that she take an afternoon off and have a little fun. He let his mind sift through all the possibilities.

Then he grinned down at the children. "Ready to go on an adventure?"

Bianca hopped up and down and clapped her hands. "Yes!"

Dieter cocked his head, as if trying to figure out how they'd gone from discussing Franz's being too old to marry Clarabelle to going on an adventure. But he seemed to contemplate the dilemma for only a moment before grinning and nodding.

Franz wasn't entirely sure of the connection himself, but he did know he was tired of holding back. For better or worse, he wanted to enjoy the day with Clarabelle and the children and deal with the repercussions another time.

11

Clarabelle couldn't stop smiling. She felt like a child again, having cast off the weight of all her responsibilities and frustrations, even if only for a short while.

And it was all because of Franz.

She was crouched beside the children along the creek bank near the simple plank bridge Eric had apparently constructed long ago. As much as Franz was trying to fit underneath, his legs still stuck part of the way out.

"Who's crossing first?" Dieter asked from beside Clarabelle.

"Maybe I should," she offered, unable to stifle the thrill of acting out the old tales that Franz loved to tell the children. She was glad now that she'd agreed to accompany the children and Franz on one of his learning adventures for the afternoon.

She really hadn't had much choice, considering how

eager and adamant everyone had been to have her join in the adventure.

The outing had helped to distract her just a little from her brooding over the fact that today was Friday and that Franz was scheduled to call upon Clementine that evening.

Clementine had been excited about it all week. As happy as Clarabelle had wanted to be for her sister, she'd only grown more morose as the week progressed. The truth was, she didn't want Franz to go to dinner with Clementine, and she'd been holding out hope he would cancel.

But it had grown too late for that, and all morning she'd been trying to resign herself to the prospect that Franz would fall in love with Clementine. It would happen in just one evening with how irresistible Clementine was.

After wallowing in frustration long enough, Clarabelle had given in to the children's and Franz's request to join them. She'd packed a simple picnic lunch, and they'd hiked out to the edge of the far hay field that bordered the woods.

She'd spread out a blanket and their fare of hard-boiled eggs, sliced ham, and bread she'd baked the day before. All the while they'd eaten, Franz had regaled them with stories.

When finished, he'd asked the children which stories

they wanted to act out, and they'd chosen the tale of Aladdin first, then the story of the three little pigs. Now they were pretending that Franz was a troll who lived under a bridge, and they were three goats needing to cross over.

"We have no grass here." Clarabelle looked around at the rocky area near them. The forest floor was covered in old pine needles and some brush.

"So we need to cross to the field?" Bianca poked her head up to peer across the creek to the hay field nearby, where they'd left their blanket and the remainder of their lunch.

"Yes, we have to go."

Dieter nodded gravely. "If we stay, we'll die."

"I don't want to die." Bianca's eyes welled with sudden tears.

Clarabelle wrapped an arm around the little girl and squeezed her. "Remember, we're only pretending, sweetie."

She nodded and gave a wobbly smile.

Dieter was frowning and eyeing Franz's legs as if they really did belong to a troll. "We should find something to give the troll. If we each give him a gift, maybe he'll let us pass."

"I like that idea." Clarabelle was truly amazed at the creativity of Franz's methods of teaching the children. Not only was he developing in them a love of literature with his storytelling, but he was fostering problem-solving skills and logic.

Dieter glanced around as though looking for something to barter. "It has to be valuable, or the troll won't take it."

"I know!" Bianca whisper-yelled. "I'll give him my shoes."

Dieter rolled his eyes. "Why would the troll want your shoes?"

Bianca looked at her shoes, then her skirt and blouse. "It's all I have, Dieter. What else can I give him?"

Clarabelle's mind was fast at work, searching for a lesson of her own she could teach the children. After all, she didn't want Franz to be the only one doing all the instructing.

"I have an idea," she whispered as she stood. "Wait here."

The two nodded and poked their heads up higher to watch as she inched toward the bridge of logs. "Hello, Mr. Troll."

"Who goes there?" Franz replied in a gruff, booming voice.

"It is I, the mama goat, and I would like to request safe passage to the other side of the bridge for my little goats."

The troll released a cackling laugh.

Clarabelle had to fight back a laugh of her own.

"Please, Mr. Troll. I am willing to sacrifice anything for my little goats. Ask whatever you wish, and I will give it to you so long as from now on you will never harm anyone who wants to cross the bridge."

"Anything?" Surprise tinged Franz's question, so much so that he forgot to use his pretend troll voice.

"Yes. Anything." She wanted to show the children that sometimes sacrifice was the greatest gift of all, no matter how hard it might be. She glanced behind her to find them peering over the rock they were hiding behind, their faces filled with worry and anticipation.

She smiled at them to reassure them that everything would be all right.

The troll was silent, probably trying to figure out what to require of her.

"Well, Mr. Troll?"

He cleared his throat almost nervously. "I have decided what I'd like."

"And what is that?"

"You must marry me and come live under the bridge with me."

She laughed and then quickly cupped a hand over her mouth.

Franz ducked out, his brows quirked. "And why are you laughing at my demand?"

"I expected that you might require me to give you my riches or make me your slave. Not that you'd marry me."

"I want a wife," he said, using his gruff voice again. "Because I am lonely and despised by all. Maybe love is what I need to change my ways."

Dieter and Bianca were smiling now too.

She began to walk toward Franz. "Very well. I'll marry you, Mr. Troll, if you promise to change your ways."

He was sitting beside the bridge now. As she approached, his gaze made a slow perusal of her body. Something in his expression spoke of just how much he liked what he was seeing.

Her skin flushed under each touch of his eyes, and warmth spread low in her abdomen, making her crave more just like it—more of his appreciation, more of his attention, more of his desire for her.

Because that's what it was. Desire flared in his eyes, and he was making no effort to hide it.

As she neared the creek bank where he waited, her steps slowed, her legs trembling with something she didn't quite understand but that also felt a lot like desire.

His jaw was taut, his lips pressed tight, and the blue of his eyes had grown darker until it was almost the color of midnight. He'd left his hat back on the blanket in the field, and now his light-brown hair was wavy and wind-tossed, as carefree and unhindered as he was.

She'd been fighting a strange attraction to him all week, but she hadn't wanted to acknowledge anything—

hadn't wanted to think about it and set it free inside her. Not with the way Clementine was gushing about Franz every time she came over.

Clarabelle pressed a hand to her chest to halt the wild pounding. Surely Franz was only playacting, didn't really desire her, and she was making more out of the storytelling than he intended.

He stood and held out a hand toward her. "Come to me, my bride." He used his large booming acting voice.

The children giggled.

Franz fought back a smile, clearly drawing life and inspiration from his audience. When she didn't put her hand in his, he wiggled his fingers in an exaggerated motion, making it abundantly clear she had no choice but to put her hand into his.

As she did so, his fingers immediately closed around hers as though he feared she might pull away. But as soon as his flesh was against hers, she couldn't think about anything else but the feel of him—the strength in his hand, the pressure of his hold, the warmth of his skin.

He didn't seem to be as affected and was nodding at the children. "Who would like to perform the ceremony of marriage?"

Dieter jumped up. "Me! I'll do it!"

Bianca was on her feet in the next instant. "No, me!"

Clarabelle was tempted to put a stop to the whole charade. After all, marriage was too sacred an institution to use in their make-believe world. But as the children rushed over, she couldn't dampen their enthusiasm. It wouldn't hurt to pretend for a little while longer, would it?

Franz led her away from the bridge until they were standing on level ground, his hand clasped firmly around hers. Dieter and Bianca stood in front of them with wide grins.

"Let us gather together." Dieter projected his voice to sound like that of the reverend, making them all laugh.

"What happens next, Uncle Franz?" Bianca asked expectantly.

"We must say our vows." He turned toward Clarabelle, his smile too handsome to resist. "Dieter, why don't you ask me if I'll have this woman to be my wedded wife, to live together after God's ordinance in the holy estate of matrimony."

Using his best imitation of a reverend, Dieter asked both Franz and Clarabelle the same question, partially botched but mostly as Franz had instructed.

Then Franz grasped both of her hands and began to recite the common marriage vow: "I, Franz, take thee, Clarabelle, to be my wedded wife, to have and to hold from this day forward, for better or worse, for richer or poorer, in sickness and in health, to love and to cherish until death us do part."

Even though this wasn't real, she couldn't keep the

flutters from fanning to life in her stomach, especially because Franz stood before her so tall and handsome and full of life and possibilities.

Whenever she'd pictured her wedding day, she'd only ever had one dream: that she be deeply in love with her groom. Nothing else—the place, the guests, her dress, the ring—had mattered.

Perhaps someday, it would end up being like this moment with Franz—spontaneous and full of joy.

"Your turn." He squeezed her hand.

"I, Clarabelle, take thee, Franz, to be my wedded husband, to have and to hold from this day forward, for better or worse, for richer or poorer, in sickness and in health, to love and to cherish until death us do part."

"It's done." Dieter stared up at them as if he really had just married them. "Now I pronounce you husband and wife."

Clarabelle knew she should tug her hands free from Franz's, but she liked the feel of their hands together too much to make the effort. And Franz, likewise, hadn't moved to release her, almost as if he liked holding her hands too.

"You need to kiss your bride." Bianca jumped up and down. "Right, Dieter?"

"I think so." Dieter shrugged. "I've seen Maverick kissing Hazel, so I reckon it's true."

Clarabelle could feel the warmth spiraling inside her

again at the nature of the conversation. She had to say no, but before she could figure out how without having to disappoint the children, Franz tugged her hand and seemed to be pulling her toward him.

He wasn't planning to kiss her for real, was he?

His eyes seemed to encourage her not to worry, that everything was all right, and that he'd be careful not to take things too far.

Of course this was still just part of the story. He was still acting, and she needed to keep acting too.

His sights dropped to her lips, as if he wasn't able to stop himself. Just as quickly, he jerked his eyes away and then leaned in so that his mouth was next to her ear. "Would you allow me a kiss on your cheek?"

His low whisper in her ear was unlike any sensation she'd experienced before and sent tingles racing up her backbone. As his mouth brushed her ear and his nose skimmed her cheek, her legs felt too weak to hold her weight, and she clutched at his vest with her free hand to hold herself up.

What was this reaction she was having to him? Her breathing turned suddenly shallow, and her pulse seemed to be thundering.

He didn't move back. "Just a little one?"

In the cascade of sensations and thoughts, she'd almost forgotten that he'd asked her if he could kiss her cheek. She knew she shouldn't allow it even in pretend, and even *just a little one*. Although she tried to force the word *no* from her lips, she found herself giving him a tiny nod of acquiescence.

He pulled back enough that he could look into her eyes. His gaze was intense, as if he wanted to make certain he'd gained her permission before kissing her cheek. It was sweet of him to be so polite about it.

That's all the kiss would be. A polite gesture. Like a friend kissing her cheek in greeting. Or like one of her brothers saying goodbye.

She tilted her head so that he had access to her cheek.

He bent down, hesitated a moment so that she could feel his exhalation against her skin.

Anticipation tightened her stomach. Before she could brace herself for more, his lips pressed gently to her cheek. Softly, tenderly, sweetly.

She drew in a sharp breath, the exquisiteness of the moment nearly making her swoon. The charming and wonderful Franz Meyer was kissing her cheek. Hers. As if she were a treasure, something rare and prized, that needed careful handling.

He lingered an extra heartbeat, as though he wasn't ready to be done. Then he shifted back slowly, his eyelashes low, his nostrils slightly flared.

Had he been affected by the kiss like she had?

"Now it's settled!" Bianca threw herself against them both, and the momentum forced them to break away from each other—although Clarabelle found herself still clinging to his hand.

"Now you're married, and you can be our new mother and father." Bianca held on to each of their legs and beamed up at them.

Dieter wrapped his arms around them, too, pushing her and Franz closer again.

Franz's gaze was riveted to her mouth, as if he wanted to kiss her again but this time on her lips.

Oh, sweet heavens. He wouldn't dare do that, would he?

The whirlwind in her stomach picked up speed. What was going on between her and Franz? Had they taken their playacting too far? Or had it already been more than playacting from the start?

Whatever the case, she had to set the children straight. The marriage wasn't official. "Hold on, children." She began to unfold herself from their grasps. "We're only pretending. Franz is just the troll, and I'm the mother goat."

Franz tore his attention away from her mouth finally, gazed in the direction of the field, and blew out a tense breath.

Was he frustrated?

Clarabelle disentangled her hand from his. And she wasn't sure whether to be relieved or disappointed when he didn't try to hold on to her longer.

He glanced at the sky and then tugged his watch out of his pocket to check the time.

She didn't need a watch to know the afternoon was spent and that they had chores waiting for them. It would soon be time for Franz to call upon Clementine. Was he thinking about that too?

Her mind filled with the vision of Clementine in her best dress, greeting Franz at the door of the ranch house. She'd be as beautiful as always.

Clarabelle blinked, trying to ward off thoughts of Clementine and focus on the look in Franz's eyes from moments ago. But even if Franz had felt something this afternoon that went beyond pretending, those feelings would soon be shoved away by all his attraction for Clementine.

It was Clarabelle's turn to release a tense breath.

Before Franz could examine her face and see the conflict there, she reached for Bianca's hand and started to lead the little girl toward the bridge. "Time to return home, sweetie."

As fun as the afternoon had been with the children and Franz, she couldn't forget it was all pretend, and that's the way it needed to remain.

12

Clarabelle stepped out of the bank and forced herself not to look down the street in the direction of Dewitt's Hotel, even though the need to see Franz was mounting with every passing moment.

That wasn't why she'd hitched the wagon and come into town with the children first thing after rushing through the morning chores. She wasn't anxious to see his face and try to gauge his reaction to his time with Clementine. Or at least, that's what she'd been trying to tell herself.

But the truth was that she'd hardly slept all night with thoughts of Clementine and Franz running through her head. On her way into town, she hadn't been able to resist stopping over at the ranch, hoping Clementine would tell her that it hadn't gone well, that Franz wasn't the man for her, and that she didn't plan to see him again.

Unfortunately, Clementine had gushed even more.

"I'm in love with him," she'd said dreamily as she stood at the stove and stirred one of the bubbling pots of a sugar-and-butter mixture. "I've finally met the man I intend to marry."

Clarabelle's heart had cracked at the declaration. And it had cracked even more as Clementine had breathlessly described everything she loved about Franz. By the time Clarabelle had torn herself away and started to town, she'd been nearly sick. With jealousy that her sister had such a lovely time with Franz? With the frustration of losing a man she'd never had?

Whatever the case, her chest still ached.

She drew in a breath of the crisp morning air, letting the coolness that lingered from the night clear her head. Forcing her attention away from the hotel, she focused instead on the wagon in front of the bank and the children waiting on the bench as she'd instructed them, having promised that if they behaved, she would allow them to each pick out something at the store once she finished her errand.

The trip to the bank had been long overdue. In his will, Eric had given her access to his account, and since she'd started running low on supplies, she had no choice but to find out what financial means he'd left her.

The bank proprietor, Mr. Paris, had checked the ledger containing information about the money Eric had deposited at the bank for safekeeping. One hundred dollars. It wasn't a fortune, but if she was careful, hopefully it would get her by until after the sales from the produce and hay.

She'd earned a little already from the eggs and milk, and she had more to sell today. But the banknotes she'd withdrawn would allow her to purchase flour, yeast, baking powder, coffee beans, and other foodstuffs along with kerosene, chicken feed, and thread for darning the children's clothing.

Before leaving, Mr. Paris had drawn her into his office and told her about a key Eric had placed at the bank for safekeeping. He'd indicated that Eric had wanted the key to stay confidential. Although Mr. Paris didn't know what the key was for, he guessed perhaps it was for a small safe that Eric may have purchased and kept at his home.

She'd debated taking the key with her, but since she hadn't seen a safe anywhere in the cabin or barn, she'd decided to leave the key at the bank where it wouldn't be lost or stolen—at least until she discovered more about what the key might be for.

She'd have to ask the children what they knew about a safe. If they didn't know anything, she'd have to search the property more thoroughly.

Regardless, she had the sinking feeling the key and safe were somehow related to Eric's murder—that whatever he'd locked away was what the murderer had wanted. After the past couple of weeks of wondering, she finally had a clue to share with Franz, who'd been doing his best to find out why his brother had been murdered.

"Did we behave well enough to get something at the store?" Bianca sat primly on the wagon bench, hands in her lap, looking almost as proper as a princess.

Clarabelle shook off the foreboding and smiled at the children. "Yes, you did well."

They smiled in return and climbed down. Worth's General Store across the street was already busy at the early hour. As she crossed with the children, her gaze strayed in the direction of Dewitt's Hotel again, even though she didn't want it to. Franz was likely still inside enjoying a hot breakfast and coffee.

Maybe by the time she finished shopping, he'd be ready to leave for the farm and would ride alongside them. Even though she wanted to see him this morning, a part of her was afraid that he'd be so far enamored with Clementine that there wouldn't be any room for affection toward her. Because that's what always happened.

Yet, was she secretly hoping this time would be different? That Franz would like her better than Clementine?

"Miss Oakley, dear," came the kindly voice of Mrs. Grover from down the boardwalk.

Clarabelle halted outside the store to find the matronly teacher hurrying toward her with her bustled skirt swishing with each step. Without school in session on Saturdays, Mrs. Grover was probably taking care of her errands too.

After exchanging hugs with the woman, Clarabelle sent the children ahead of her into the store and chatted for a few minutes with Mrs. Grover, catching up on how school was going, how the various children were coming along with their lessons, and the possibility of a recess for a week or two.

"I should go . . ." Through the front door, Clarabelle caught sight of Bianca and Dieter, who seemed to be remembering to use their manners with the storekeeper as well as the other customers.

Mrs. Grover's smile faded, and a furrow formed between her brows. "I suppose you haven't heard about the rumors?"

"Rumors?"

Mrs. Grover glanced around as if to make sure no one was listening, then she dropped her voice. "About you and Franz Meyer."

"What could anyone possibly have to say about us?"

"Quite a bit, I'm afraid."

Something fluttered in Clarabelle's chest. She wasn't sure if it was trepidation or anticipation. It had to be trepidation, because she surely didn't want people gossiping about her and Franz, did she?

Mrs. Grover must have taken the silence as

permission to continue. "With him riding out to the farm and spending every day with you alone, well . . ."

Clarabelle supposed his daily visits could be taken as more, but the children were there with them constantly, so they were chaperoned to some extent.

"Mr. Grover thinks it's best if Franz cuts short his time here in Colorado before your reputation is ruined entirely." Mrs. Grover's expression was grave. "And I have to agree. I'd hate to have parents refuse to allow you to return to teaching at some point because they believe you're . . . tainted."

At the insinuation, Clarabelle dropped her head, too embarrassed to look the dear woman in the eyes or anyone else passing by. "I assure you, Mrs. Grover, nothing untoward is going on between Franz and me." As much as Clarabelle disliked Franz courting Clementine, maybe it was for the best after all.

Even though Clarabelle had enjoyed his company and help around the farm, he had to be more careful about how much time he spent with them. Apparently, she needed to have a conversation with him today about the rumors, no matter how unpleasant and awkward it would be.

As the door of the general store opened, Mr. Irving stepped out onto the boardwalk and gave a slight bow. "Good morning, ladies."

As the solicitor situated his tall top hat on his head, he

towered above them.

Before Clarabelle could return the greeting, Mr. Irving was speaking again. "I hear congratulations are in order, Miss Oakley—or should I say, Mrs. Meyer?"

Congratulations? Mrs. Meyer? Clarabelle could only shake her head.

Mrs. Grover's mouth dropped open, and she stared at Mr. Irving for several moments before turning to Clarabelle. "You're married to Mr. Meyer?"

Mr. Irving cocked his head toward the store. "According to the children, there was even a kiss at the end of the ceremony."

"Well, why didn't you say so, dear?" Mrs. Grover patted Clarabelle's arm. "That solves all the problems, and we have nothing to worry about."

Drats. Clarabelle peered through the glass in the doorway again to find Dieter and Bianca browsing the shelves and behaving . . . except they were telling everyone about the pretend wedding yesterday.

Mr. Irving smiled, his eyes bright with what could only be described as relief. "I'm certainly happy to know the situation has resolved itself. I never did like the idea of you running the Meyers' place by yourself."

"I've been doing well."

"Of course you have. But it's only fair now that Franz should take over for his brother. Don't you think?"

Mrs. Grover squeezed Clarabelle's arm and smiled.

"With Franz managing the farm, you can return to assisting me again at school sooner rather than later. And we needn't worry about your reputation. Isn't that lovely?"

Panic was closing its fingers around Clarabelle's chest. She had to clear up the misunderstanding before everything spiraled out of control the same way it had when Eric had proposed marriage. "I'm sorry for the misunderstanding, but I can explain."

"Tell Franz to stop by my office soon." Mr. Irving began to stride away from the store toward his office. "I'll need to add his name to the official documents."

"That won't be necessary," she called, but Mr. Irving was already waving to another passerby and exchanging greetings.

"Now, dear." Mrs. Grover patted Clarabelle's cheek like she often did the students. "It'll be for the best. That Franz seems like such a nice young man. And handsome too. I'm sure in no time at all you'll grow to care for each other."

For heaven's sake. She had to set Mrs. Grover straight. "We did have a wedding yesterday, but it was just with the children—"

"That's fine. Sometimes a small wedding is better anyway, especially when it's more of a practical arrangement."

"But that's just it. It's not practical."

Mrs. Grover's finger tapped against Clarabelle's lips and smiled secretively. "It's okay if you already have feelings for each other. But let's keep that between you and him, shall we?"

Clarabelle clamped her lips closed. She was only making matters worse every time she opened her mouth. If only she could learn to be more forceful in saying what she meant.

But here she was again, unable to voice her true thoughts. Soon enough, everyone in town would believe she was married to Franz, and then what would she do?

As Mrs. Grover congratulated her again, Clarabelle's mind reeled, and all she could think about was the need to get out of town. First she had to enter the store and at least gather the children. She could only pray that no one else would say anything to her about her supposed marriage to Franz.

She had no such luck. Every single person in the store wished her well in her new marriage. Mr. Worth even added a jar of pickles to her order as a wedding present.

By the time she exited the store, she was so mortified that she was speechless. All she could do was force a smile at the well-wishers and hurry the children along to the wagon.

Only after the wagon was loaded and they were well away from town and nearly home did she finally find her voice. The children hadn't spoken the whole way home either, and she guessed they'd sensed that something was bothering her.

She wasn't angry with them, but she did want them to know they'd been wrong to speak falsehoods. Unless they hadn't realized the marriage yesterday was only part of their playacting. But hadn't she and Franz made that clear enough?

As the wagon bumped along, she took a breath, then spoke as calmly as possible. "Children, you shouldn't have told everyone that your uncle and I are married."

On the bench beside her, Dieter exchanged a glance with Bianca, then hung his head.

"You do know the ceremony yesterday was only pretend, don't you?"

"I think it was real," Bianca said as if she were somehow an expert on the matter. "Reverend Livingston told us that it matters what's in a couple's heart."

"When did you see the reverend?"

"While you were in the bank," Dieter mumbled.

Clarabelle shifted the reins in her hands, directing the horse to turn down their lane. "I'm sure Reverend Livingston told you that he's the one to officiate weddings."

Bianca shook her head. "No, the reverend said he doesn't have to be there."

"It's true," Dieter added, sitting up but still looking guilty. "He told us that since 1877, common law marriages are legal in Colorado and don't need a license, documents, or anything else to be real so long as the couple agrees on the union."

"And you said your vows and agreed." Bianca smiled up at Clarabelle. From the innocence in her eyes, the little girl obviously didn't understand the repercussions of all that had happened.

"We were only pretending, sweetie."

"That's what I told her," Dieter said. "But she insisted you and Uncle Franz were really married."

"They are." Bianca's lip jutted out stubbornly.

Clarabelle expelled a breath. "What's done is done. Now we'll just have to figure out a way to clear up the confusion."

"Do you think Uncle Franz will be mad at us?" Dieter was peering ahead, his gaze fixed upon the man in question, who was kneeling next to the garden fence and fixing a loose spot where rabbits had been squeezing through and eating the newly sprouted beans.

At the sound of the wagon lumbering down the lane, Franz sat back on his heels and glanced in their direction. He didn't seem happy or eager to see them. Maybe he'd already heard the news. And maybe after last night with Clementine, the rumors about being married had been difficult to hear.

Clarabelle gripped the reins tighter, wishing she could turn around and go the opposite direction, but she was on a collision course with disaster. She couldn't prevent the inevitable crash and could only pray no one would get hurt.

13

He had to tell Clarabelle the truth.

Abandoning the hammer and fence, Franz pushed himself up from the ground and dusted his hands on his trousers.

He didn't want to confess that he'd had dinner with her sister the previous evening, but all throughout the time at High C Ranch, guilt had nagged him. With every horse and rider that had passed by the house, he'd imagined Clarabelle and the children stopping by and finding him at the table alone with Clementine, having dinner by candlelight.

Although Clarabelle was gracious, she would wonder why he hadn't mentioned it. Maybe she would even be hurt and suspect he was sneaking around behind her back.

The truth was, he wasn't interested in Clementine.

Of course, Clarabelle's twin was a lovely young

woman. She'd gone to a great deal of effort for the meal. And she'd been pleasant.

He might have even had a decent time if he hadn't been worrying about Clarabelle's discovering what he'd done. He hadn't intentionally hidden the plans from her, but he also hadn't spoken of them.

Now what would she say when she found out?

The wagon rattled down the lane, drawing close enough that he could see the tension in Clarabelle's body and the firm press of her lips.

What if she'd gone to her family's ranch or crossed paths with Clementine already this morning and learned of his deception? Was it even deception?

He released a puff of air, but at the same time couldn't stop from straightening his bow tie and then his hat.

The irony of his predicament wasn't lost on his sensibilities. He'd spent the past six years denying he wanted a woman or marriage. He'd convinced himself he would remain a bachelor. He'd even believed himself to be entirely content with his life and work.

But within moments of meeting Clarabelle, everything he'd thought he'd known had been turned upside down. Now, honestly, the only thing he wanted was her.

Holding her hand yesterday and kissing her cheek hadn't helped in the least. His thoughts and his dreams last night had been filled with the sensations touching her had evoked—the softness of her skin, the scent of her hair, the intake of her breath. He kept reliving the moment his lips had made contact with her and the sweet yearning that had filled him and seemed to have taken up residence inside him.

He didn't know what to do about all that he was feeling for her, but he did know he had to tell her about the dinner with Clementine. He just hoped he was able to inform her first before she learned of it elsewhere.

As the wagon rounded the cabin and lumbered toward the barn, he ambled in their direction, his feet slower than usual.

"Hi, Uncle Franz." Bianca waved at him, her face wreathed with her usual smile.

Dieter, however, focused on the barn ahead, his forehead creased. Although Clarabelle shot Franz a glance, she, too, seemed to be avoiding him.

This wasn't what he'd hoped for.

Franz reached the wagon as it halted in front of the barn. From the bags and crates in the back, it was obvious she'd gone to town and purchased more supplies.

He should have done it for her, should have realized she might have needs that he could help with. But of course, he wasn't accustomed to thinking about the basics as he had always left those details to the servants.

Had he ever overlooked things with Luisa?

In the middle of reaching for a grain sack, he paused. He'd always had a good relationship with Luisa, and she'd never complained about anything. But what if he'd had faults that might have driven her away? He'd always blamed Eric for enticing her, and he'd blamed Luisa for being unfaithful and fickle.

But maybe he hadn't been kind and caring enough. Or maybe he'd been too selfish and proud. He'd certainly battled those sins over the past years as he'd tried to mature and grow into a better professor.

He could admit he still had a lot of growing to do. But at least at this point in his life he was more aware of his shortcomings, and he wanted to be a better man in a way he never had before.

"Uncle Franz." Bianca was the first to stand. "I think you should know that you're married."

He smiled. "And I suppose you are still goats?" The children had internalized the make-believe too much yesterday. He would have to be more careful in the future to keep the mood lighter. He wasn't sure what he'd been thinking when he'd arranged the marriage ceremony with Clarabelle in front of the children.

That was the problem lately. He wasn't thinking clearly around Clarabelle. Or at least, he wasn't thinking with his head and was instead letting his emotions rule him.

"Of course we're not goats." Bianca scoffed as he

helped her off the wagon bench and steadied her on the ground. "But the reverend said you and Clarabelle are married."

Franz arched a brow at the child. How was he supposed to respond to such a nonsensical statement?

Dieter jumped off and landed beside the girl, wary, as if anticipating a reaction.

Clarabelle descended and, still avoiding his gaze, reached into the back of the wagon and lifted out one of the grain sacks.

"I will carry it." He started around the wagon.

"It's not overly heavy." She hustled forward into the barn.

He chased after her. "I would like to."

Her shoulders were stiff, and she didn't stop to smile at him like she usually did. Something *was* wrong. She *had* heard about his dinner with Clementine and was upset at him.

He dodged a chicken, then reached for her arm and halted her before she could go too far. "Wait, Clarabelle. I would like to apologize." He took the grain sack from her arms.

Although she relinquished it, she didn't turn to face him. "No, I should be the one to apologize to you." Her voice held a note of frustration. At him? Or herself?

The children had moved into the open barn door and were watching the interaction.

"Children, unload the wagon and take anything into the house that belongs there." He spoke firmly, expecting their obedience the same way he did with his students. While he might have unconventional teaching methods, he considered mutual respect to be just as important as creativity.

Dieter nodded, reached for Bianca's arm, and then began to lead her away.

Once the children were no longer in sight, Franz set the bag of feed on the ground and gently turned Clarabelle to face him. Even then she kept her focus on the hay and the lingering chicken that was strutting around their feet.

"I apologize," he said softly. "I should have told you before going."

She lifted her eyes, and the green was dark and filled with confusion.

He hesitated. She was offended over his dinner with Clementine, wasn't she? Or what if she didn't care whether he'd called upon her sister?

For a moment, he was tempted not to say anything more, but he had to finish the conversation he'd started. "Clementine invited me for dinner last night, and I went."

"*She* invited you?" Clarabelle didn't seem too taken aback, more curious.

"Yes, she invited me to pay her a call. Perhaps it was

to make another young man at the store jealous. I cannot rightly recall. But I never should have agreed to it."

"Really?" The one word came out breathless and filled with hope.

"Yes, I regret it." He stuffed both hands into his trouser pockets, afraid he'd reach for her—something that seemed to be happening all too easily lately.

"Clementine made it seem as though you'd asked to call on her."

His thoughts halted. "So you knew about the dinner plans?"

"Yes, Clem told me earlier in the week."

"I see." So he'd worried for nothing.

"I stopped by the ranch this morning, and she said she enjoyed your time together."

"Your sister is a very lovely woman. But . . ."

With her eyes riveted to him expectantly, she worked at her bottom lip.

Of course, as always when he considered her lips, he wanted to bend down and take possession of them for himself. But he couldn't.

"But . . ." she prompted him.

He made himself look away from her to settle his thoughts. Did he dare tell her why he hadn't enjoyed his time with Clementine? What harm could come from being honest? "The truth is, she is not you, and so I had no interest in spending time with her."

"Really?" Light flickered in her eyes, and the corners of her mouth curled up into the hint of a smile.

He'd intended to tell Clementine that he had no plans to call upon her again, but as he'd been readying his horse to leave, Maverick had come out of the barn, and he'd lost the opportunity to speak privately with her. He hoped she'd picked up on his cues that he saw her as nothing more than a friend, but if there was any confusion on the matter, he'd have to let her know next time he saw her.

He moved a step closer to Clarabelle, earnestness and need driving him. "I have loved getting to know you, Clarabelle."

"But Clementine is more exciting and talkative than me."

"No one can compare to you." His voice came out softer and more passionate than he'd intended.

Instead of welcoming his compliment, her brow furrowed. Did she doubt his sincerity?

He knew exactly how to convince her he was telling the truth. He could pull her into his arms and steal a kiss—this time without asking.

What would that accomplish except to make the future more confusing? He was still in the same dilemma. He wasn't planning to stay in Colorado. Not when he had responsibilities and work he loved awaiting him back home. And he'd already decided he couldn't ask her to give up everything after knowing him such for a short time.

She dropped her gaze to the sack of chicken feed near their feet. "I'm afraid you won't think so highly of me after you learn what happened in town today."

"I am sure it cannot be too bad." He doubted anything could change his feelings for her. The emotions burning through him had already seared him too deeply, and that realization scared him more than a little.

"It's pretty terrible," she whispered.

His breathing stilled.

"The children told everyone we got married yesterday."

That was all? He drew in a breath and almost laughed at his relief. "That does not sound like something too terrible."

She kept her gaze trained on the grain bag. "The terrible part is that I didn't correct the misunderstanding."

She hadn't? Why? Anticipation swirled inside him.

"I admit I'm not good at being confrontational or saying no." Her voice was laced with embarrassment. "And once everyone started congratulating me, I didn't know how to tell them they were wrong."

"I see." He felt strangely let down but wasn't sure why. Maybe because he'd hoped she wanted him? But instead, she'd just been shy.

She dug the tip of her boot into the hay, twisting back and forth as though waiting for him to say more.

He hesitated and then said the words he knew he must. "It should be easy to clear up the confusion."

She lifted her lashes, her gaze guarded. "Do you really think so?"

"I can ride into town later and explain what happened yesterday."

"You can tell everyone we don't really have a common-law marriage."

"Common law?" He wasn't familiar with what that meant or the laws of Colorado or of America.

"The reverend said it's legal now in Colorado to have a real marriage without a pastor or papers or anything. As long as the couple agrees that they're married, then they are." She was watching him carefully now, clearly trying to gauge his reaction to this news.

His mind was moving sluggishly, and all he could think about was the possibility that he might be married to Clarabelle—that she might be his wife and he might be her husband.

"The children told everyone we exchanged our vows . . . and that we kissed."

He wanted to deny that the vows or kiss had meant anything to him, but when he'd been standing there in the forest yesterday speaking the words to love and cherish her until death parted them, he'd wanted his promise to mean something. On some level, he supposed he'd orchestrated everything because he wanted to have her.

Her wide eyes were full of innocence as she waited for him to present a solution to their current dilemma.

But what if he didn't want to find a solution?

What if this woman was meant to be his? What if this meshing of their lives—of their magnetic fields—was inevitable? Perhaps he'd even been drawn across the continents and oceans for this very reason.

Or he was going crazy.

He exhaled a taut breath, pivoted away from her, and rubbed at the back of his neck. He was overthinking the situation, and he needed to do the honorable thing by correcting the misconception that he and Clarabelle were married.

"Not to make matters worse," she said quietly, "but people were already spreading rumors about our being together."

"I had heard the same." From the sheriff. He hadn't wanted to believe the sheriff, but obviously the situation with Clarabelle had escalated very quickly, and now he had to figure out a way to repair her reputation.

"I'm truly sorry, Franz." Her voice held remorse. "I didn't mean for things to get out of hand."

"It is not your fault." Before he could think of anything else to say to ease her mind, a winded Dieter stumbled into the barn, dragging Bianca with him. His eyes were frantic.

Franz's pulse spiked, and his muscles tensed.

"The house." Dieter gasped for a breath. "Someone broke in and made a mess of everything."

14

Someone had been inside their home.

The thought pummeled through Clarabelle as she waited outside the door with the children. She had her arms around each one, tucking them safely against her body. Even so, Bianca hadn't stopped shaking.

Franz had made his way slowly through the cabin, his pistol out and ready to fire, and was now rumbling around the loft where the children slept.

Clarabelle appreciated that he was taking precautions and trying to keep her and the children safe, but she suspected that whoever had ransacked the place was gone by now.

And it was ransacked. Every piece of furniture was overturned, cushions and pillows off, rugs thrown aside, drawers and trunks emptied, and even some of the floorboards had been pulled up.

Had Eric's murderer been back and done this? Who

else could it have been?

It had to have happened after she'd gone into town with the children this morning. She hated to think that meant someone had been watching her every move and had waited until she'd left before coming into the cabin.

On the one hand, she was relieved the break-in hadn't occurred while they were home and could have been hurt. On the other hand, it meant Eric's killer was nearby—or had been in the area again. And that was a frightening thought. Especially for the children, who'd only just stopped worrying about their father's murder and the danger lurking around them. They hadn't climbed trees and dropped blankets on visitors since Franz's arrival.

But now . . . this would stir up their fears again.

Franz hopped down from the ladder that led to the loft. If she hadn't been so nervous, she might have appreciated seeing the sliver of skin at his waist as he lifted his shirt and slipped his gun back into the holster hidden underneath.

He picked his way through the wreckage to the door. When he ducked outside into the sunshine, he shielded his eyes with his hand and scanned the perimeter of the property as if he were hoping to catch a glimpse of the intruder.

Of course, nothing moved, not even the leaves. Everything was still and silent in the morning, as if nature were slumbering and would awaken later during the heat of the day.

Franz stepped off the stoop. "I will check the barn." He started to lift his shirt again and reach for his gun.

"No, Franz." She released Dieter and clasped Franz's arm. "What if someone is there?" She shuddered to think that, just moments ago, she and Franz had stood in the barn discussing their marriage situation.

She wasn't entirely sure if they were married or not. They hadn't really come to a solid conclusion, had they?

Regardless, she didn't want Franz to put himself in danger. She had only to think about how she'd found Eric in the field with a battered and bloody head to know that the peril was real.

Franz paused and glanced around again. "I will feel more secure if I make sure I have checked everywhere."

She clung to him more tightly. "Please. Stay here with us."

With a furrowed brow, his gaze came to rest on her. He seemed to be warring with what to do. "I should probably go into town and let the sheriff know about the attack. But I did not particularly like him yesterday."

"My pa always said that Sheriff Shade keeps control but doesn't always keep the law."

"Your pa sounds like he was astute."

"He was a good man." Clarabelle swallowed the lump that sometimes still surfaced when she thought about losing her pa so abruptly.

"We could use a few good men to help us right about now."

"I could go get Maverick."

Franz was still peering around the farm cautiously.

"My brother Ryder has a ranch near Frisco. I could go after him too." Both Maverick and Ryder would ride over and help her in a heartbeat. And so would Tanner if he were home. Or maybe Tanner wouldn't come if he knew Ryder would be there. The two had been at odds over the winter and hadn't been speaking to each other since then. She'd tried to talk to Tanner about it the last time he'd been around in May, but he'd refused to discuss it.

Franz released a long breath. "If only I knew what the murderer was after."

Was it possible someone was searching for the safe—if that's really what Eric had hidden? Or maybe the attacker was trying to find the key.

"Eric might have a safe hidden somewhere out here."

"A safe?" Interest lit Franz's eyes. "Tell me more."

She relayed all she'd learned from the banker earlier in the morning about the key and the banker's insinuation that the key might be for a safe. With the new knowledge, Franz plied the children for any memories they might have of their father purchasing a metal box, but neither could recall anything of the sort. The children also had no memories of their father digging a hole and burying anything.

They spent the rest of the morning cleaning the cabin and putting it back to order. After a light fare for lunch, Franz suggested searching the property. Clarabelle hesitated, not wanting to venture too far from the cabin. But she felt safer with Franz—and so did the children—so they followed after him, helping him look for any clues that might lead them to a hidden safe.

Of course, as with everything, Franz turned the search into an educational experience. And after some time of playing his witty games, she could sense the children relaxing and losing the fear that had plagued them since finding the cabin broken into.

Even so, all through the evening chores and supper, the children didn't want to be alone. Franz stayed later than usual to help tuck them into bed, reading them story after story from one of the books he'd purchased in town, until finally he climbed down the ladder.

She rose from the sofa, where she'd been patching a hole in Dieter's trouser legs. With the open style of the loft, she'd been able to listen to Franz reading while sewing and had enjoyed his renditions of the stories as much as the children.

"They are finally asleep," he whispered as his feet touched the floor.

"Thank goodness." At least for now, Bianca was asleep, but Clarabelle wouldn't be surprised if the little girl woke up with more nightmares later.

"It's gotten late." Franz glanced at the windows. Though she'd pulled the curtains, the darkness outside penetrated the cabin, casting a gloom that even the bright lantern light couldn't dispel.

She hoped no one was lurking in the nearby woods or field and watching the house again, but she shuddered at the prospect anyway and wrapped her arms across her middle.

Franz crossed to a knitted blanket on the sofa, retrieved it, then draped it over her shoulders.

His fingers lingered on her shoulder for a moment before he stepped back. "How is that? Better?"

She wrapped the blanket tightly around her and nodded. "Yes. Thank you."

He picked up his hat from a peg beside the door but hesitated putting it on.

She'd kept him too late. "I'm sorry that now you have to ride back to town in the darkness."

"You will lock the door after I leave?"

She nodded, but all the trepidation from earlier in the day came rushing back. If the killer wanted to get inside, would he break a window? Was she really safe staying by herself? "Maybe I should go back to High C Ranch tomorrow and live with Maverick for a while."

Franz fidgeted with the brim of his hat. "Yes. At least until we know more."

"I'll do it tomorrow night."

He nodded, continuing to bend his hat. "That is good. But I am not comfortable leaving you and the children alone here tonight."

She smiled at him, hoping to put him at ease. "We'll be fine one more night." At least, she prayed so.

He hung his hat back up on the peg, then squared his shoulders and faced her. His hard, curved jaw was more chiseled than usual. "I cannot go."

"It's all right. I don't want to impose."

"No, I will not be able to ride away and have any peace."

She knew she ought to protest more adamantly, but she couldn't force the words she needed to say—that it was completely inappropriate for them to stay together in the same house all night unchaperoned.

It wouldn't be proper, and the rumors about them would only increase, especially once Franz attempted to clarify that they weren't really married.

"Are you sure?" She had to voice some caution, didn't she?

"I will sleep on the sofa." He nodded to the small—and uncomfortable—piece of furniture that was frayed and worn.

She shook her head. "You can take the bed. I'll sleep on the sofa."

"I will be fine out here."

"It's the least I can do to repay you for your kindness."

"I am the one who should be repaying you."

She laughed lightly. "You're too nice to me."

"You deserve to have someone to dote on you and spoil you."

"See. There you go again." Already the fear that had gripped her was loosening.

"How about if we determine who gets the bed in a friendly game of checkers?" He cocked his head toward the checkerboard that sat on the side table.

"I must warn you that I'm a checker champion." She returned to the sofa and lowered herself to her familiar spot.

She loved the distraction of the checker game and realized soon enough that he was letting her win on purpose. When she confronted him about his strategy, he gave her an endearing grin so that she didn't have the heart to scold him.

All the while they played, he told her more about his childhood and the types of games he used to play with Eric and his father. Every time he shared more about his past, she could picture him as a boy and young man with his family, having adventures at his home near the lake that he so fondly talked about.

"If you and Eric were so close," she said as she reclined her head against the sofa after winning another game of checkers—at least her tenth in a row, "why did he move to America?"

Leaning his head against the sofa, too, Franz suddenly tensed and shifted his attention to the checker piece in his hand.

"I'm sorry." She sat up, the blanket sliding from her shoulder. "I shouldn't have probed. You don't need to discuss it with me."

He leaned forward and tugged the blanket back up so that she was covered again. "It is not a good tale."

She settled her hand over his where it rested on the sofa. "Not all of our stories are good. But perhaps we need the tragic tales to make us appreciate the happy ones all the more."

She began to move her hand off his, but he flipped his hand over and circled her fingers with a strong and warm presence—one that felt right and safe. Even though a part of her warned against sitting on the sofa holding his hand this way, another part of her wanted to enjoy this moment with him and worry about the consequences later.

"I met Luisa when I was twenty and she was nineteen," he started.

"Eric's Luisa?"

Franz's lips curled into a wry smile. "She was once *my* Luisa."

"Oh." Suddenly, she knew the direction the story was about to take, and she didn't like it.

He was staring unseeingly at the stove, the door

glowing with embers left from when she'd cooked supper. "Her father was a baron, similar to mine—"

"I didn't know your father was a baron." She wasn't entirely sure what that meant but guessed it was some high-ranking German nobility, which meant Franz was likely a nobleman of a privileged and wealthy class that far surpassed her status.

"I do not think about the nobility much anymore and have done away with the titles associated with my family name. It is easier at the university that way."

"I see." In some way the news of his nobility didn't surprise her. Not with how educated and proper and gentlemanly he was.

He was silent for a long moment, then started his tale again. "I visited Luisa's home one break with her brother, who was a friend from school, and it did not take long for Luisa and me to begin courting. We were engaged a year after that."

Clarabelle hadn't known Luisa well, but she did remember her dainty features and beautiful smile. "She was very pretty."

Franz nodded solemnly. "I loved her—or at least I thought I did."

Although a part of her wanted to be jealous of Luisa for winning Franz's affection, Clarabelle's heart felt heavy for the part of the story Franz had yet to tell.

"Sometimes, on my school breaks, she visited me at

my family's home in Neubrandenburg, at our estate on the sea. While there, she got to know Eric." His voice took on a hard edge. "I did not think anything of their friendship until one time I returned home and discovered she had come early to be with Eric."

Clarabelle squeezed his hand, but he was no longer present in the cabin. He was back in his family's home.

"They did not know I had returned." He paused, as though searching for the right words. "I walked in on them together in Eric's bed."

Clarabelle couldn't stop her sharp intake at the indecent—and bold—remark. She had the sudden vision of Franz standing in the doorway of the bedchamber and the two lovers lying together, completely entranced with each other and unaware of the heartache they'd caused Franz.

She knew no words could take away the ache, so she did the only thing she could think of—she laid her other hand on top of his.

"I broke the engagement." His voice was low and filled with pain. "I told Eric and Luisa I never wanted to see either of them again."

She stroked his hand, needing to comfort him and wishing she could heal his wounds.

He paused his tale and drew in a breath, seeming to dig for the strength he needed to finish. "Eric came to the university several weeks later to tell me he and Luisa were getting married, that she was carrying his child."

"Oh, Franz." Tears pricked her eyes at the hurt he'd gone through. "I'm sorry."

He intertwined his fingers through hers, sliding them together tightly. "He renounced his claim on the estate, gave me his title as baron, and took only a pittance of his inheritance. Because of the scandal and shame, her family disowned her and gave her nothing."

"So they came here to get away from the disgrace?"

He nodded.

How different life must have been for Eric and Luisa in America compared to what they'd once known. It had probably been a difficult adjustment full of hardship, especially being so far away from family.

Franz glanced around the cabin as though recognizing the same thing.

Even if life hadn't been easy for Eric and Luisa, they'd always seemed happy. At least, whenever she'd seen them. But of course, she wouldn't say that to Franz. "Eric mentioned he'd written to you but that he hadn't heard back. Now I understand why."

Franz hung his head. "Before leaving, Eric begged me to forgive him. But I told him I never would."

"You were hurt and angry."

"After six years of hanging on to the hurt and anger, I knew it was time to come here, talk to him, and let it go."

"I admire you for having the courage to do so."

His gaze lifted then to hers, and his handsome face with its lean and striking lines was etched with deep regret. "I was not courageous. I waited too long."

"But you're here—"

"After arriving in Colorado, I delayed in Denver one week. One week, Clarabelle." His grip on her hand tightened. "If I had let go of my bitterness sooner and come earlier, even just one week earlier, I might have been here to save his life."

"You don't know that."

"Now I have to live with the knowledge that my unforgiveness had a role in his death."

His reasoning was unfair, but how could she convince him of that? "You didn't have control of Eric's life or death. Even if you'd been here, the murderer could have come and killed him when you were in town or while you were sleeping—or maybe even killed you too."

He was quiet for a moment. "I know, logically, you are correct. But it still does not take away the fact that I sensed he was in some kind of trouble from his letter, and I wanted him to pay for what he had done to me."

She didn't want to offer him any trite platitudes. After the deaths of her pa and ma, she'd never liked when people tried to comfort her with reminders that her parents were in a better place or that she'd learn to adjust to life without them.

She'd simply needed someone to listen and

understand that, even if her guilt was irrational and illogical, she still felt as if she could have done something to prevent her parents' deaths, especially her ma's.

"It's good you came." She spoke gently, hoping he would sense that she cared. "You might not be able to ask Eric directly for forgiveness, but you can still ask it of God and for yourself."

"Perhaps you are right."

"Hopefully by the time you leave, you'll have made peace with all that happened in your past."

"It will help if I can find justice for him."

A scream pierced the air, coming from the loft.

Breaking the connection with her, Franz jumped to his feet, his gaze darting around, his hand fumbling under his shirt for his pistol.

She rose more slowly, weariness settling over. "We're not in danger. It's just Bianca. She's having another nightmare."

15

Franz brushed a hand across Bianca's cheek.

She released a shuddering breath, but her eyes remained closed.

Was she asleep again?

Her little frame was curled up and motionless on her bed, which was built into the wall on two sides and low to the ground, allowing him to kneel beside her and comfort her.

When he'd first heard her screaming a short while ago, he'd assumed the intruder was back in the house and was up in the loft hurting her.

Thankfully, no one had been there. Nonetheless, Bianca had been frantic with fear that someone was prowling about the loft.

Franz had assured her many times that no one was there and that he'd protect her, but she hadn't calmed down until he'd started telling her one of his stories. One story had turned into two, until finally her eyes had closed and she'd fallen asleep again.

Now he backed away carefully so that he didn't awaken her. On the bed across from Bianca, Dieter lifted his head, giving Franz a grateful look.

Franz patted the boy's arm before starting down the ladder. As his feet touched the floor, his gaze went directly to Clarabelle with the need to reassure himself she was safe.

She sat on the sofa beside the lantern and was sewing again. "Thank you," she whispered, appreciation radiating in her expression.

"Does she have nightmares often?" he whispered back as he crossed to her.

"She was having them every night after Eric's death, sometimes multiple times in one night." Clarabelle whispered her reply too, obviously not wanting to chance waking Bianca again either. "But she was getting better, even slept through the night a couple of times recently."

Franz could only imagine how frightening everything was for a little girl Bianca's age. To have her father murdered was horrible enough, and now to have this attack on the home made matters worse.

Franz took his place on the sofa. Clarabelle had already removed the checkerboard, and although he wanted to close the distance between them, he was afraid that if he sat too close, he'd frighten her with his ardor, and she'd make an excuse to get up.

He'd liked holding her hand before and wished he could recreate that moment. But she didn't put down her mending, and he knew he didn't have a right to reach for her hand anyway. He hadn't made a commitment to her or offered her a future—not that she'd asked for one with him.

But he couldn't start facilitating closeness with her if he hadn't decided upon his intentions. And after the marriage mix-up in town today, he wasn't exactly sure what to do. While he'd told her he would clarify their situation with the townspeople, a part of him didn't want to. He wanted to allow the misconception to become true and make Clarabelle his.

In fact, the desire to be with her had grown stronger over the evening. In telling Clarabelle about Luisa, something seemed to have loosened in his chest—something that made him feel freer than he had in a long time.

Clarabelle was a good listener and compassionate and wise.

More than that, however, he sensed his sharing about Luisa had helped him see more clearly that what he'd experienced with Luisa hadn't really been love. Whatever it had been paled in comparison with the depths of his feelings for Clarabelle.

Maybe losing Luisa to Eric had actually been the best

course. Maybe she'd ended up with a person she could connect with more than him.

Not that he wouldn't have worked hard to have a good marriage with her. His father had set a fine example of what it was like to be a loving husband, and he would have done all he could to make his marriage to Luisa happy. Ultimately, they hadn't truly been meant for each other.

"The rings you wear," Clarabelle said softly. "Would you tell me about them?"

He didn't realize he'd lifted his hands to his chest and the chain underneath his shirt until she looked pointedly at his fingers fidgeting with the outline of the rings.

"They were my parents' wedding rings. Wearing them makes me feel like they are still with me. I know that sounds strange—"

"No, it makes you sound sentimental."

He smiled at her kindness. "And sentimental is a good thing?"

"Yes." She smiled back.

He loved everything about her, but he especially loved that he could talk to her about anything. He settled into the sofa, and for a long while they conversed about so many different things that he felt as if he'd known her months instead of days.

When Bianca woke up later with more screaming and crying, he went up again. It took longer to calm her, and by the time he finished and came down, Clarabelle was slumbering on the sofa under the knit blanket.

For a moment, he stood beside her and allowed himself to watch her, taking her in without having to hold back. Strands of her hair had come loose from her plait and curled over her smooth, pale cheek. He wanted to reach down and finger that strand and then make a trail over her face, around her chin, and up to her lips.

She was so beautiful his chest ached just looking at her.

She'd likely allowed herself to fall asleep there in order to force him to take the bed. But he wasn't planning to let her win, especially since she'd been waking up with Bianca for so many nights. The least he could do was rest on the sofa and get up with the little girl if she had any more nightmares, giving Clarabelle the chance to sleep well.

Gently, he bent and scooped Clarabelle up into his arms. As he settled her against his chest, her lashes lifted, revealing her green eyes, hazy with sleep. "Franz, what are you doing?"

"Putting you in bed where you belong." He headed toward the bedroom off the back of the cabin.

"No—" A yawn interrupted her protest.

He entered the dark room, two more steps already bumping him into the bed.

"Franz, please," she said, but her voice was weary.

He lowered her to the mattress, and thankfully she didn't resist.

Instead, she settled in and drew the knit blanket around her body. "I'll comfort Bianca next time," she whispered.

He finished tucking the blanket up to her chin. "Do not worry about it. I will take care of her."

With the faint light coming in from the main room, he saw her lashes fall and sleep claim her again, so he straightened and stepped back.

"Thank you," she said, her voice husky.

What he wouldn't give to hear her talk like that to him every day. As tempted as he was to keep talking to her, he forced his feet to walk out of the room.

He didn't trust himself to stay a moment longer.

He lost count of how many times he climbed into the loft to calm Bianca. Finally, after one particularly intense nightmare, he came down to find Clarabelle standing at the bottom of the ladder.

"You've been awake most of the night, Franz." She hugged the blanket around her. "Let me go up and tend to her next time."

He couldn't deny the exhaustion that was settling in, so when she guided him toward the bedroom, he was too tired to resist. He didn't bother checking his watch, but he guessed dawn was only an hour or two away. He needed to get a couple hours of sleep so that he had the energy and stamina for continuing the search for whatever Eric had hidden.

And after the attack on the cabin yesterday, he also needed some rest if he hoped to stay alert and at his best.

He fell asleep almost right away but awoke every time Bianca started screaming and sobbing. He went up once to find Clarabelle on the floor, rocking back and forth with the child on her lap, tenderly showering her face with kisses.

Clarabelle had whispered at him to try to get more sleep, and reluctantly he went back to the bedroom and lay down again.

The next time he awoke, Clarabelle was hovering above him and attempting to pull a blanket over him.

"How is she?" he asked.

"Now that it's daylight, I think she's finally asleep."

The room had lightened, and from what he could tell past the curtain in the room's only window, the sun had risen.

He shifted and began to sit up.

She pressed against his shoulder. "No, don't get up. I'll take care of things."

As she took a step back, he clasped her hand. "Let me."

"No, I'm up and awake already." She yawned but didn't pull away from him.

"But you are tired."

"So are you." Her eyes were troubled. If she felt anything like he did, then she was at a complete loss as to how to help the little girl.

He tugged at her, causing her to stumble closer to the bed. "At least sit down for a minute and talk to me about Bianca."

She hesitated only a moment before perching on the edge of the box board that held the mattress.

"Has she been like this before?" He pushed himself up and situated his back against the wall.

"No." Clarabelle's voice held a note of defeat. "She's never woken up more than two or three times in a night. Not even that first night after Eric's murder."

"Perhaps she is even more anxious after what happened to the cabin."

Clarabelle's shoulders slumped, and they shook just a little.

Was she crying?

He laid a hand on her back.

She stiffened and sniffled.

"What are you thinking?" he asked gently.

"She needs a better mother than me, Franz." Her voice wobbled.

"That is not true. You are a good mother."

"I don't know why Eric chose me." The words came out on the edge of a sob.

"Because you are wonderful with the children."

"He should have picked someone else. Someone older and wiser and more capable." Her voice cut off with another sob.

"Nein, mein Liebchen." He leaned forward and drew her into a hug. He didn't care that they were on a bed and that physical contact wasn't appropriate for them. All that mattered was comforting her.

She buried her face against his chest, and the sobs came freely, quiet but broken.

He wanted to say more, needed to convince her she had all the qualities Bianca and Dieter needed in a mother. But he sensed that right now, after the past night of trying to console Bianca, Clarabelle needed to let out her tension and frustration.

As her sobs finally began to calm, he situated himself against the wall again, drawing her into the crook of his arm with her face still partially buried against his chest. With one arm around her back, he simply held her.

That seemed to be enough. No words were necessary. After a moment, she quieted and didn't move, just rested against him as if she'd found peace in his arms.

He hoped so. He had the overwhelming need to take care of her and make her life better and easier and happier. That's all he wanted to do. He wanted to spend the rest of his days being with her and making sure she always had something to smile about. He wanted to love her and spoil her and sacrifice for her.

As impossible as it seemed in such a short time, he'd fallen in love with her. Maybe it had been at first sight. Maybe there was a rational, scientific reason behind it. Or maybe there was no explanation at all.

Whatever the case, he loved her with a consuming depth that was so pervasive his chest radiated with it. And he knew that he could never live without her. He would give up everything and stay in Colorado if that's what it would take to be with her. Surely he could find places to teach here, even in the mountains.

He had to find a way to be with her and make a future together work. Of course, she probably didn't feel quite the same way he did. It might take some time and wooing and convincing to be able to win her heart, but he would do it eventually. He'd work hard, be patient, and show her she meant everything to him.

Her breathing had evened to a slow and rhythmic pace, and her eyes had closed. Had she fallen asleep?

He had to sit up, get off the bed, and allow her to sleep. But as he shifted forward, she released a soft, tired sigh.

He paused. It wouldn't hurt anything to let her sleep for a few minutes against him, would it? After the nearly sleepless night she'd had, he didn't want to wake her up.

The chores could wait. The children would likely sleep late.

Suddenly, he wanted nothing more than to hold her for a little longer. He'd just sit with her and rest.

Slowly, he reclined against the wall again. She didn't resist and seemed to curl into his side as if she were made to fit there.

He bent his head and buried his nose in her hair. He took a deep breath, inhaling the sweet scent of sunshine and strawberries. She smelled so good. And she felt so perfect against him.

Even though a part of him warned against staying on the bed for too long, he closed his eyes and breathed out a sigh of contentment. He was exactly where he wanted to be for the rest of his life . . . by her side.

16

Clarabelle awoke with a start, the distant call of her name lingering in her memory. Was someone looking for her? Or had she just dreamed it?

Her eyes felt heavy and her head groggy, and as she struggled to open her eyes, strong arms tightened around her.

Wakefulness swept through her, and she was suddenly conscious that she was lying down on a bed beside someone. Her eyes flew open to find herself looking into Franz's sleeping face on the pillow beside her.

Bright sunlight streamed through the window, leaving little doubt that she was indeed in bed beside Franz.

How had this happened?

She scrambled to find an answer, but she couldn't think past the blur in her brain. It didn't matter how she'd ended up there—she needed to get up immediately. Before he roused and realized she'd joined him in bed. Or maybe he'd slipped in beside her.

She shifted back just a little and realized her hands were flattened against his shirt and his chest. She could feel every hard muscle and even the solid beat of his heart. How had she dared to be so bold as to let herself touch him this way?

A flush worked its way into her cheeks.

She had to find a way to slip out of the bed without waking him up. But how could she do that with his arms surrounding her? What would Franz think when he awoke to find her there?

"I could wake up like this every day." His whisper was gravelly.

She jerked her sights from his chest back to his face to find that his eyes were still closed, but his lips were slightly turned up in the beginning of a satisfied smile.

He wasn't upset they'd somehow ended up like this?

Her memory spun back to the last few moments before she'd fallen asleep—the long and difficult night and how she'd stumbled into the bedroom, exhausted and in tears. He'd been so kind and tender with her.

He'd likely been as weary as she'd been, and they'd succumbed to much-needed sleep.

With his eyes closed, she admired his features: his lean cheeks, his hard, carved jaw, and his distinguished chin. His hair was scattered and messy, the sunshine turning the light brown to a pale wheat color. A shadow of unshaven scruff made him even more handsome.

As she let her gaze trail across his mouth and its solid lines, the hint of his smile faded away. And beneath her hand, she could feel his heartbeat pound harder and faster.

When she lifted her gaze, she found herself peering into eyes that were blue and clear and bottomless. Why did his features have to be so appealing?

Ever since he'd arrived, she'd tried not to stare at him, tried not to focus on how handsome he was, tried not to let herself become swept into his piercing gaze. Now, with the full force of that blue pulling her in, she didn't want to resist any longer.

What was he thinking? He'd said he liked waking up like this. But what did it mean? Did he like being with her?

"I can see all those questions in your eyes." He held her gaze for a second longer before his eyes made a trail around her face, starting at her forehead, moving to her nose, then jaw, and lingering on her cheek. Was he remembering that he'd kissed her there on their wedding day?

His gaze came back to her eyes. "May I answer the questions?"

She nodded.

He leaned his head closer to hers, and his hand on her back drifted up her spine.

The feathery touch of his fingers sent a cascade of pleasure tingling over her skin.

As he bent in further, her heartbeat began to race. When his lips softly touched against hers, she didn't know what to think. What was he doing? He'd said he'd answer her questions. She'd assumed he'd say something, but maybe she'd been wrong.

His hand on her spine shifted higher to her neck, and as his fingers touched her bare skin above the collar of her shirt, she gasped. But his lips pressed in at that moment, capturing the gasp, capturing her mouth, and capturing her soul, all at once.

His lashes fell, but not before she caught a glimpse of the darkening desire there.

Oh, sweet heavens. He was really and truly kissing her on the mouth. The gentleness and the sweetness of his lips against hers sent that same pleasure swirling deeper into her body, so that like him, she closed her eyes, the pure bliss of the moment overwhelming her.

His hand upon the back of her neck seemed to be guiding her head to just the right angle for the kiss, and his lips tugged at hers so tenderly that she forgot to breathe.

She was kissing Franz Meyer. She, Clarabelle, who'd never had the attention of a man, much less had one want to kiss her. How was this possible?

He broke away slowly, as if he wasn't quite ready to

do so. He didn't move very far back, still close enough that she could feel his breath upon her lips.

She didn't open her eyes and didn't move. She wanted more from him, but she wasn't sure how to express that.

"Did I answer your questions?" His voice was low and did strange things to her belly.

She lifted her lashes to find that his face was still close enough that their noses were almost touching. She tried to read his eyes, tried to make sense of what he was saying. But she was too lost in his nearness and the sensation of the kiss he'd just given her to understand anything else.

"Since you are still confused"—his whisper was charged with something she couldn't name—"I must clarify again."

This time when he closed the distance, she was ready. She was eager for his lips to touch hers again, and she rose up to meet him.

As his mouth came against hers, he pressed in harder and more fervently.

Her heart sped, her breathing quickened, and need swelled within her, a need she hadn't known she had—the need to be close to Franz, to be a part of him, to connect with him more completely.

The passion of his kiss invited her to join in the melding, so she let her lips tangle with his. And she was surprised when he took the kiss even deeper, sweeping in like a summer storm, engulfing her with pouring rain, with lightning crashing through her, sizzling along every nerve ending, leaving her body heated and charged and eager for more of him.

Even with the power of his kiss and the power of his body against hers, she sensed a restraint in his movements and muscles. The realization that he was being careful, that there was more that could be unleashed between them, made her tremble.

His hand had slipped from her neck to her hair, which had somehow come unbound over the night and now hung in tangled waves. His fingers were smooth and gentle, and yet, even as they wound through her hair, he seemed to be holding himself back there too, as if he wanted so much more than he was allowing himself.

He broke the connection of their lips and shifted away.

This time she wanted to chase after him and nearly whimpered her protest.

But her entire body was blazing, and she was suddenly keenly aware of just how intimately their bodies were touching—their hands on each other, every part of her body flush against him.

Somewhere at the back of her mind, she sensed that she needed to put even more distance between them, but the connection with him pulled her in so strongly and thoroughly that he was all that existed in her world and nothing else mattered.

"Clarabelle." He spoke her name reverently.

She also sensed a request in his tone, that he wanted her attention, and so she opened her eyes and met his gaze again, feeling suddenly shy about how she was reacting to his kisses.

He drew his hand from her hair to her cheek, tracing a path down to her chin. His eyes were so dark the blue had turned to midnight. "I love you."

She couldn't keep from inhaling a sharp breath. He loved her? How was that possible already?

"I know it is soon," he whispered. "But I have never been more certain of anything."

"I don't understand how."

"I do not completely understand it myself." His whisper was so soft it was almost a caress. "All I know is that I have been in love with you since the moment I met you."

Her heart swelled with such affection for him that she wanted to tell him she loved him in return. But how could she be certain he was the man she'd been dreaming of, the man who would be her other half, the man she would cherish until her dying day?

He bent in and brushed a kiss against her forehead.

The touch contained his adoration. Could he really love her already? Was it possible?

Whatever was happening between them, she wanted more of it. She couldn't stop herself from stretching up and brushing her lips to his again, tentatively, not sure if he would welcome another kiss or if he'd already had his fill.

He responded immediately with a soft moan that told her he most certainly welcomed her kiss, that he was as hungry for her as she was for him. Perhaps even more so, because this time, he ravaged her lips with a passion that seemed to unbridle more desire. His fingers in her hair tightened, and his palm on her spine splayed against her possessively.

A part of her already knew she was his. From his first kiss, he'd claimed her, and she didn't want anyone else. But someone calling her from a distance penetrated through her haze. Was that one of the children?

She needed to get out of the bed before the children saw them together in such an intimate way. It would only make matters more complicated. Or would it?

"Clarabelle?" The voice came again but louder.

Franz must have heard the call at the same time she did, because his deep kiss turned shallow. And although he didn't release her, he paused.

"Heaven have mercy, Clarabelle!" The shocked declaration came from right behind them. "Have you no decency?"

The voice belonged to Clementine.

Clarabelle froze.

Franz was the first to break away. He rolled back, releasing the kiss and his hold on her body.

Her pulse began to tap with dread. She'd put Clementine completely from her mind since yesterday—hadn't thought about her since Franz had admitted in the barn that he hadn't enjoyed the dinner.

Maybe those hadn't been his exact words. But he'd made it clear that he hadn't fallen under Clementine's spell, that her charm hadn't worked on him, that he had no intention of being with her again.

When he'd said as much in the barn, Clarabelle had been almost giddy with the realization that Franz hadn't fallen for Clementine.

But . . . that didn't change the fact that Clementine had fallen for Franz. And now what would she think to find them in bed together, not just resting but kissing passionately?

"What exactly is going on?" Clementine's tone held confusion . . . and hurt. "I came to see if you needed help getting the children ready for church, and this is what I find."

Clarabelle didn't want to turn over and face her sister. She wanted instead to bury her face into the pillow and hide.

However, Franz was sitting up and gently assisting her up too. She could feel him looking at her, probably wanting to assure her that everything would be all right. But the dread inside was turning into an avalanche—like the one that had killed her pa—sliding down and growing more intense with every passing moment.

"This is my fault," Franz said as he stood. "I should have remained on the sofa instead of coming in here."

Clarabelle pushed up from the bed as well. "And I shouldn't have sat down on the bed that last time I came in."

Clementine, in her best Sunday gown, was frozen in the doorway, her gaze bouncing between them before landing upon Clarabelle and staying there.

Clarabelle smoothed down her skirt, trying not to think that only moments ago, Franz's leg had been tangled in it. Just like his hand had been tangled in her hair. She rapidly brushed a long strand out of her face, the mass falling around her as if announcing her guilt.

The guilt was probably written all over her face. Guilt at having been caught in an improper situation with Franz, but also guilt because she hadn't talked with Clementine first before letting herself finally admit she liked Franz.

"You told me you weren't interested in Franz." Clementine's voice rang with accusation.

Franz quirked a brow.

Clarabelle couldn't meet his gaze. She was interested in him and had been from the start, but she hadn't been able to deny Clementine's excitement and desire for Franz. Yes, she had a hard time saying no to people, but she had an even more difficult time saying no to Clementine.

Clementine braced her hands on her hips. "From the looks of things, you sure have gotten cozy with Franz."

Clarabelle took a step toward her sister, wanting to calm her down before everything escalated. "This is the first time. I vow it."

"You should have just told me. Instead, you were sneaking around behind my back."

"We were not sneaking." Franz spoke firmly.

Clementine glared at him. "You could have been honest with me the other night when you came calling instead of leading me on."

"I did not intend to lead you on. I had planned to inform you I would not call on you again, but I did not have the chance."

"Or maybe you were too much of a coward to tell me."

"That is not true." Franz combed his fingers through his hair. "I am in love with Clarabelle, and I am not afraid to let everyone know it."

"In love with Clarabelle?" Clementine's wide eyes came to rest upon Clarabelle. Surprise filled them along with anger.

Clarabelle forced herself not to cower. Why was it so

surprising that a man should love her? She wasn't so unappealing, was she?

Clementine shook her head, as though the thought of the quiet and reserved twin winning a man was simply too unbelievable. "And do you love him too?"

Did she? After kissing, the emotions that were swirling through her were even more unfathomable than before.

"You do." Clementine's voice wobbled as she spoke.

"I . . ." Clarabelle wanted to deny her sister, but how could she? What if this was love that she had for Franz?

"You should have been honest with me, Clarabelle. I even asked you if you were okay with me seeing Franz, and you told me you wanted me to be happy."

"And I do want you to be happy."

Clementine waved at the bed. "If you'd been honest, then maybe I wouldn't feel so betrayed right now."

Betrayed. The word settled over the room and over Clarabelle's heart. "I'm sorry."

Clementine spun and half ran, half walked toward the front door, which stood wide open.

Clarabelle raced after her. "Wait."

Her sister only stalked faster, moving out of the house and down the steps toward her waiting horse.

"Please, Clementine. I don't want you to be angry with me."

"Maybe you should have thought of that when you

decided to get into bed with Franz." Clementine reached her horse and tugged the lead line free of the branch where she'd looped it.

Clarabelle clutched her sister's arm, wanting to work things out before she left.

"No. Don't." Clementine jerked herself free and then lifted herself into the stirrup. "I don't want to hear any more of your excuses."

They'd never fought before—or at least, not more than simple squabbles. They had to work this out, couldn't leave hard feelings to fester between them. Not like Franz had with Eric.

Clarabelle's pulse slowed. What if that happened? This was a similar situation. Franz had even caught his brother and Luisa together in bed. The two had kept their relationship hidden from Franz instead of being honest. And in the end, they'd betrayed and hurt him terribly.

What if Clementine felt as betrayed? As devastated? What if she could never get over it? What if she harbored bitterness for years the same way Franz had?

Clarabelle reached for her sister again, but Clementine was already situating herself in the saddle.

"I never meant to hurt you."

Clementine shifted her mare around but then halted and shot Clarabelle a look that contained all her anguish. "You did hurt me, Clarabelle. You hurt me a lot."

With that, Clementine nudged her horse down the

lane and rode away without looking back. As she turned onto the road and disappeared from sight, Clarabelle's legs began to shake.

What had she done? Was her relationship with Clementine ruined?

She cupped a hand over her mouth to hold back a cry of dismay only to find that her cheeks were wet with tears.

17

Franz steadied Clarabelle. She was trembling, and he wanted to pick her up and cradle her against his chest.

But he'd already been bold enough for one morning. More than bold. He'd made a terrible mess of things.

If only he hadn't allowed himself to fall asleep holding her on the bed. But he'd loved having her in his arms. He'd loved the closeness. And he'd loved that he could comfort her.

He'd told himself he would just rest for a few minutes, but with how tired he'd been, he should have known that would turn into much longer.

At the very least, when he'd first felt her rousing, he should have made himself get right up and walk away from the bed and all the temptation she posed with her warm body, sleepy voice, and unfettered hair.

But he supposed he wouldn't have been able to tear himself away even if he'd given himself a hundred lectures on why it was a bad idea to keep holding her. A part of him wondered if he would have been able to tear himself away from kissing her if they hadn't been interrupted by Clementine.

He wouldn't have done more than kiss her. At least, he wanted to believe that. Guilt nagged him nonetheless, along with the realization of how easy it was to lose control. He'd always thought Eric had been weak for not showing restraint with Luisa, and he'd always believed himself more self-controlled, maybe even more righteous than Eric.

Yet all it had taken was one time kissing Clarabelle, and he'd already pushed himself beyond what was appropriate. Even if some people believed he was married to Clarabelle, and even if common-law marriages were legal, they hadn't truly made a commitment to each other yet. Yes, he'd said he loved her, and he'd meant it. But he still didn't have a right to lie on a bed with her and kiss her until they were both senseless.

Perhaps, in losing control, he wasn't much different from Eric after all. At the very least he shouldn't have stood in judgment on Eric and Luisa and cast them out the way everyone else had. The two had likely needed the support and love of family during those early days of their marriage and pregnancy instead of the ostracism.

Silence settled over the grassy cleared land around the cabin, with only the chirping of a nearby chickadee to remind him that life went on. The sun was already high, the sign that the morning was well underway, and none of the chores had been done. From what he could tell, the children were still asleep, or at least had remained inside during the commotion.

Clarabelle wavered again as she stared in the direction Clementine had gone. Tears now streaked her cheeks. She was a sensitive woman, and her sister's frustration had upset her.

But in his opinion, Clementine had overreacted. Aside from having dinner with her the one time, he'd never given her any reason to believe he cared about her or wanted to have a relationship with her. Even while he'd been at the dinner, he'd tried to keep their conversations and interactions formal and polite.

In the end, what Clementine thought or wanted didn't matter. His heart was already taken. Yes, he should have made a point of informing her sooner that he wouldn't be calling on her again, maybe should have told her he was interested in Clarabelle.

Interested didn't even begin to describe how he felt about Clarabelle.

Even though he'd declared his love privately to her, and now publicly in front of her sister, she hadn't yet spoken of her love for him. She was most certainly attracted to him. He had no doubt of that anymore. Not after the way she'd kissed him back.

But attraction didn't equate with love.

Just because he was already in love with her didn't mean she would fall instantly in love with him. Most people didn't fall in love at first sight the way he had, which meant he had to give her more time, had to be patient, had to allow for a natural progression of their relationship.

Regardless, he needed to find a way to comfort and reassure her. He reached up and brushed his thumb across a tear on her cheek, wiping it away.

Another one rolled down to take its place. "She's never been angry at me like this," Clarabelle whispered. "What if she hates me the same way you hated Eric?"

Why was Clarabelle comparing herself to Eric? Surely she didn't think their being found in the bed was like what had happened when he'd discovered Eric and Luisa. "The situation this morning is very different from my relationship with Eric."

She turned her big green eyes upon him. "I betrayed my sister, Franz. I should have talked to her first before allowing myself to . . . to be with you."

"You do not have to get her permission to care about me."

"But she likes you, and I came in and stole your affection away from her."

Franz spun Clarabelle gently so that she was facing him. "You did not steal it away from her. You could not do so—not when you have always had it."

"But she asked me if she should cancel her plans to see you, and I didn't say no. I told her if seeing you would make her happy, then I wanted that for her."

He was beginning to understand Clarabelle's relationship with her twin. Clementine was more dominant and had likely always been the leader of the two. And Clarabelle had probably gone along with her sister, rarely speaking her mind or demanding her way.

That sort of sibling relationship might have worked for picking out toys and candy when they were children, but the dynamics didn't apply for choosing men now that they were adults.

Franz wanted to tell Clarabelle again that it wouldn't matter how much permission she gave to her sister to see him. It wouldn't matter how happy Clementine would be with him. He didn't want her. He only wanted Clarabelle.

But at the moment, she wasn't able to see that. Instead, she was too worried that her relationship with her sister would turn out like his had with Eric. "Clementine is much kinder and more loving than I am," he said. "She won't make the same mistake in despising you that I made in despising Eric."

"You don't know Clementine the way I do."

"But I also know that I was very stubborn in hanging on to my hurt." Maybe it had taken him time to come to that conclusion, but he was finally able to see it. If only he'd seen it earlier.

"Clem is stubborn too."

He reached for her hand, needing to connect with her.

Before he could circle his hand around hers, she pulled away and took a step back. "I think it's best if we don't pursue anything right now."

He could feel he was losing her. He needed to prevent it, but he didn't know how. "Please, do not push me away. We can work through this, can we not?"

"I don't know."

With her uncertainty, he could persuade her to be with him. She'd admitted that she rarely said no, which meant he could probably get her to agree to anything he wanted.

But was that really what he wanted? To coerce her? To have her feel obligated to him? To have her get tangled into an agreement the same way she had with Eric?

He shook his head. No, that wasn't how he wanted to win her over. He wanted her to be agreeable on her own. He wanted her to be willing to be with him. And he wanted her to say yes because she meant it—not simply because she didn't know how to refuse him.

"I'm sorry, Franz." She straightened her shoulders. "I already lost my pa and ma. I can't bear to lose a sister too."

"She might be upset temporarily, but you will not lose her." At least, he hoped not.

As if hearing his unspoken thought, Clarabelle's eyes saddened. "I can't take the risk of ending up like you and Eric."

Protest rose swiftly inside again, but he swallowed it. He couldn't argue with her. Instead, he had to release his intense need and wait patiently for her to be ready for him. He'd continue to build a relationship, even just a friendship, if that's all she was willing to give him. All that he knew was that he couldn't let go of her. Not yet.

But even as he tried to convince himself that he could win her and that everything would be all right, she lowered her head and walked back toward the cabin, each step heavier than the last, as if she were already thrusting him away.

18

Clarabelle knelt beside her ma's grave. Her heart ached, but she'd already spent all her tears over the past week since the fight with Clementine.

"Oh, Ma, I miss you." She'd plucked the weeds around the headstone, and she'd placed a small bouquet of early-blooming columbines on the grave.

The small graveyard just outside of Breckenridge was situated in a clearing with aspens standing guard nearby and a wrought-iron fence to keep out the wild animals. Mostly, tall grass surrounded the grave markers of various shapes and sizes, some covered in moss and vines.

Ma's marker sat next to Pa's, both of modest size and both still smooth and untouched by time and weather.

She plucked at another weed. "I hurt Clementine a lot, and she still doesn't want to talk to me."

Before riding over to the cemetery, she'd gone over to the ranch to visit with her sister. It was late enough in the day that Clementine was home from selling candy in town. But as with the previous days when she'd tried visiting and talking with Clementine, she'd gotten nowhere. Clementine was even more upset after hearing the marriage rumors.

Clarabelle had tried to clarify that she and Franz weren't really married, but Clementine had bitterly complained that Clarabelle had made her look like an even bigger fool for having dinner with Franz.

Yesterday, Franz had gone to Reverend Livingston and attempted to clear up the confusion and the rumors about being married to her. Apparently, everyone had learned he hadn't returned to the hotel but had stayed the night at the farm. Naturally, the town folk—including the reverend—assumed he was now sharing a bed with his new wife.

Franz had tried to explain to the reverend that they weren't really married—that the children had misspoken and the supposed marriage ceremony had been acting out a story.

The reverend had asked Franz some pointed questions about the nature of their relationship, and Franz had admitted to having slept together in the bed. Even though he'd made it clear that they hadn't consummated their relationship, the reverend had also made it quite clear to Franz that if he wasn't already married to her, he needed to rectify that as soon as possible.

So Franz had come back to the farm after the visit with all his bags loaded upon the horse, and his forehead had been furrowed with distress lines. He'd apologized to Clarabelle for making the situation worse.

She couldn't blame him, not when she was the one at fault for not having put a stop to the rumors the moment she'd heard them outside the general store. It was just one more incident when her not speaking the truth had caused problems.

If only she'd been braver and had spoken with Clementine earlier.

But what would she have said? What was the truth in regard to Franz? That she loved him?

He'd been at the farm all week, but he hadn't said anything more about his love for her, and he certainly hadn't tried to join her in the bed again. Not that she'd expected him to. Instead, he'd made a bed of blankets on the floor in the main room of the cabin.

Even so, just the thought that they'd been in bed together made her flush. And the trouble was, she thought about those delicious moments with him far too often. The way she'd felt so cherished and secure and safe in his arms. The way his body had felt against her. The way his mouth had taken possession of hers.

She couldn't deny she'd loved every second of kissing and holding him. She also couldn't deny that she wanted to kiss and hold him again.

Therein was the problem. He wasn't hers to kiss and hold. He'd been Clementine's, and she'd stolen him away.

Well, maybe *stolen* was a harsh word, but the fact was, she shouldn't have kissed, held, or done anything else with Franz until she'd confessed her feelings to Clementine.

The evening shadows were growing longer, and the sky was turning more colorful, with hints of lavender and rose and gold. There was still another hour before dusk settled and the children needed to go to bed. Even so, she'd been gone from home long enough.

A yawn pushed for release, but she swallowed it. Even if the living situation wasn't ideal, she was grateful Franz had helped again with calming Bianca at night—had even brought her down to sleep on the sofa several times, which seemed to settle her down a little.

Clarabelle bent and pressed a kiss to the earth and the new grass finally beginning to grow over the freshly dug dirt. "I love you, Ma. All I want is to have a relationship like you and Pa had. I was hoping maybe I could have that with Franz, but I can't do it if it hurts Clementine."

She couldn't, could she?

As soon as the thought flitted into her mind, she pushed it aside. "She won't forgive me." Clarabelle sat back on her heels and peered at the mountains that rose in the distance, the rugged peaks still holding snow even though the days had grown warmer. "I don't know what else to do."

Was she still talking to her ma, or was she now praying to God? Either way, she needed help.

For now, all she could do was bury her feelings for Franz. He'd only just come into her life. She hardly knew him. And soon he'd leave. As special as he'd become to her even in so short a time, she couldn't throw away the special relationship and bond that she'd had with her twin for her entire life.

With a sigh, she stood, brushed the grass and soil from her skirt, then made her way outside the cemetery gate to her horse. The ride to the farm went quickly, and as she started up the lane, she spotted Franz with the children in the yard beside the cabin. He'd attached one end of a rope to a large, sturdy tree branch and tied the other end to an old wagon wheel. The children were sitting on the rim as he pushed them in a large, dizzying circle.

With their heads back, their laughter rang out, greeting her with bittersweetness. She'd grown to love the children dearly over the past weeks that she'd been their caregiver. But as attached as she was becoming, they belonged with Franz. They were his niece and nephew, and they needed him and the connection with family more than they needed her.

She slowed her mount, trying not to look at Franz but

unable to stop herself from admiring his strength as he wound them around, the muscles in his arms straining against his shirtsleeves. He'd discarded his hat, and the rays of the evening sun turned his hair to a pale brown, making him more dashing than usual.

If only she'd never been attracted to him to begin with. But she was attracted. Very much so.

Her attention fell upon his smiling lips—those lips that had hungrily kissed her, giving her a taste of the pleasure she'd never known, a taste that had only made her realize what she'd been missing and that she wanted it again.

As his gaze homed in on her, his smile dimmed, became more forced.

She'd wounded him when she'd walked away from their relationship. She hadn't wanted to hurt him any more than she'd wanted to hurt Clementine, but somehow she'd ended up doing it anyway.

Her heart ached, and a part of her wanted to avoid him and the awkward exchanges they'd had since their kisses. But the children had noticed her and began to wave and call out greetings, giving her no option but to ride toward them.

When she reached them and dismounted, they excitedly asked her to watch as Franz gave them another push. They begged her to try the new swing too. Reluctantly, she sat down and allowed them to push her.

Franz just leaned against a nearby tree and watched with a soft smile—one that was finally genuine, that warmed her heart.

When only a few rays of the setting sun lingered, they finished the last of the nightly chores before heading inside the cabin. She helped Bianca wash up and get into her nightdress. All the while, the little girl began to tremble, the darkness of the night having somehow become her enemy.

Franz believed that, eventually, Bianca would outgrow the anxiety and be able to function more normally again. But the nights with her weren't easy, and as Clarabelle tucked the child into her bed, she prayed that tonight would be better.

At a sudden loud rapping against the door downstairs, Bianca sat up with a start, her eyes rounding with terror. Thankfully, they hadn't had any more scares or threats, but they'd still been fearful all week.

Clarabelle peeked over the railing to the sitting room as Franz approached the door cautiously, his revolver already out. Surely an attacker wouldn't knock on the door.

He leaned against the door and spoke in a low voice. "Who is there? Please identify yourself."

Whoever was on the other side spoke so quietly that Clarabelle couldn't hear the name, but she did hear when he said, "May I come in?"

Franz glanced up at her, his brow quirked.

"Who is it?" she whispered.

"He says his name is Jericho Bliss, a Pinkerton agent."

The name sounded familiar, and her mind scrambled to place it. Was Mr. Bliss the agent who'd helped her brother Weston out of a dangerous situation the previous Christmas? If so, Weston had nothing but positive things to say about him.

Mr. Bliss lived down in the Fairplay area. What was he doing up in Summit County?

Franz was watching her, seeming to understand without her explaining anything that she didn't feel threatened. Did Franz know her that well already that he could read her emotions?

In the next moment, Franz opened the door, letting in a fellow wearing a dark coat and a Stetson over brown hair. Lean but muscular, he carried himself with assurance and a determined set to his shoulders.

He slipped inside and quickly closed the door behind himself, as though wanting to stay hidden, or at least not let anyone catch him coming into the cabin.

Something in the keen way he glanced around told her that he was seeing every detail and that nothing missed his attention. And something else told her that he was there for only one reason: because of Eric's murder.

As she climbed down the loft ladder, Franz crossed to assist her the last of the distance like he always did whenever he was present. She didn't need his help getting down, but he treated her like a lady, rushing to her aid, getting her anything she needed, and making sure she was comfortable.

She'd realized that he wasn't acting or trying to impress her. No, he'd treated her kindly from the moment he'd met her and showed no signs of waning in his thoughtfulness. If anything, he'd only grown more attentive to her needs.

"Thank you, Franz." She offered him a grateful smile as he steadied her.

Although he didn't smile back, his eyes held an adoration that made her insides melt. Her insides had been melting more frequently when she was around him. At times, she almost felt permanently liquified, as if she'd never return to being solid again.

"Mr. and Mrs. Meyer?" Mr. Bliss was watching them now, seeming to take them in as carefully as he had everything else in the cabin.

How should she respond to his assuming they were married? Since everyone else in town regarded them as a married couple, maybe it was best not to correct Mr. Bliss.

"I am Franz." Franz held out a hand and greeted Mr. Bliss with a handshake. "And this is Clarabelle."

She was amazed at Franz's smoothness in working out the awkward situation. But it shouldn't have surprised her that he was suave and well-mannered, since he was a nobleman.

Mr. Bliss nodded politely at her before pulling an envelope out of his interior pocket. "I just got this letter from your brother Eric today."

"Today?" Franz said at the same time she did.

"Yes, he sent it to the Pinkerton Agency in Chicago." Mr. Bliss slipped a paper out of the envelope. "Of course, they forwarded it to me, and the moment I got it, I rode up here from Fairplay."

"How long ago did Eric write it?" Franz asked.

"March."

Franz pursed his lips together grimly.

Clarabelle's mind quickly calculated the passing of time. Was that also when Franz had gotten his last letter from his brother? Franz had told her about the urgency the letter had contained, as if Eric had known he was in danger but had been too afraid to mention the details, similar to what she'd experienced when he proposed to her.

Mr. Bliss took off his hat and nodded at Franz. "I'm sorry for his loss. I learned of it today when I arrived in the area."

"Then you also learned he was murdered?"

"Yes. I regret I didn't get his letter and request for help right away."

"May I read the letter?" Franz asked, perching his

spectacles upon his nose.

Mr. Bliss was already handing it to him.

Franz unfolded it. Instead of reading it first by himself, he shifted, slipped his arm behind Clarabelle's back, and drew her against his side. Then he held the letter between them, so that she could read it at the same time he did.

A part of her wanted to stand on her toes and press a kiss against his cheek to show her appreciation for how kind he was. No one had ever looked out for her needs quite like him. Or maybe she was so used to always taking care of the needs of others—especially Clementine—that she'd neglected herself.

Whatever the case, she huddled over the letter with Franz. Eric's broken English was difficult to read, especially with his messy handwriting, but the message was soon clear enough. Eric had uncovered a counterfeit money operation in Summit County. He had solid proof. And the information was in a safe he'd hidden.

19

Franz could hardly see in the early dawn light, but he trudged behind Mr. Bliss as they followed the path of a stream uphill.

They'd already been hiking for the better part of an hour toward the place where Eric had buried the safe—near a waterfall in Elk Gulch—but the darkness and the mountainous terrain had made the quest more difficult.

Franz had suggested they wait until full daylight, but Mr. Bliss had said that he couldn't take the chance of anyone seeing them out exploring. He'd insisted secretiveness was the key to busting the counterfeiting operation—that if just one person of the many involved learned he was in the area, they'd hide their presses, dies, and tools so that he'd have no evidence of their crime.

From what Franz had gleaned in the conversations he'd had with Mr. Bliss earlier in the night, counterfeiting had become a national problem—one so big the Treasury

Department had created a special agency, the Secret Service, to help uncover the counterfeiters. But with the fake money production so widespread, they'd also enlisted the help of Pinkerton detectives.

For the past year, officials had known that a counterfeit operation was going on up in the high country, but they'd never been able to get anywhere. So Mr. Bliss was hoping Eric's safe would finally contain information that would be useful enough to uncover the identity of the culprits.

Mr. Bliss suspected Eric's murder was related to the counterfeiting, but he didn't exactly know how. It was possible Eric had stumbled upon the machines, or perhaps he'd been given counterfeit bills himself that had eventually led him to the operation. Whatever may have happened, one thing was certain. The people in charge had felt threatened by Eric and had decided to eliminate him before he could involve the law.

During the course of the night, Franz had told Mr. Bliss everything he'd learned so far too, which hadn't been much—the key in the bank, his suspicions about the sheriff's visit, and then the home being vandalized.

"Do you think whoever ravaged the cabin was looking for Eric's safe?" Franz asked as he climbed up a narrow trail after Mr. Bliss.

Mr. Bliss gave a curt nod. "If your brother has solid evidence that could ruin their operations, then they'll be wanting to destroy that.'"

"Or perhaps they seek the key to the safe?" Franz's breath was growing more labored with each step up the mountain.

"Maybe." Mr. Bliss hiked the mountain trails easily, as if he'd been doing so for some time. "Although, it's not difficult to break into most safes that still use keys."

Of course, Eric wouldn't have understood the intricacies of a criminal life. He'd always been an honorable man. Even when he'd made the mistake in sleeping with Luisa, he'd offered to marry her and take care of her.

It was likely he'd gotten the safe soon after moving to the high country because he'd wanted a place where he could put the gold and silver coins and other valuables he'd brought with him from Germany. And he probably hadn't trusted that a bank would be a secure enough place for anything but a key.

Mr. Bliss halted and pulled out Eric's letter again to study the details of the hiding place and the simple map. He held up his lantern, which barely had enough of a flame to give them any light, but so far Mr. Bliss had led them effortlessly over the rocky terrain, in spite of the loose stones and roots of trees threatening to trip them.

Franz drew in a breath of the chilly air. The morning so far was silent, with only the crunch of their footsteps to echo in the air. No one else was out at the early hour, not even the wild animals.

Even with all the secretiveness, Franz's heart pattered with worry for Clarabelle and the children. He hadn't wanted to leave them behind, but he also hadn't wanted to drag them out into the wilderness in the darkness of pre-dawn.

Mr. Bliss insisted that no one had followed him out to the farm last night, and he'd also claimed that no one was behind them when they'd hiked away from the cabin on their search for the safe.

All Franz knew was that he'd rather put himself in danger than allow anything bad to happen to Clarabelle and the children. His mind was still filled with the image of Clarabelle stepping out of the bedroom as he and Mr. Bliss had prepared to leave. She'd been in her nightgown but also had a blanket draped around her for modesty's sake. Her hair had been in a single long plait, and her eyes had been heavy with sleep.

As she'd gathered a sleeping Bianca from the sofa, she'd looked so enticing that he hadn't been able to stop the heat from shooting through his gut. Or the overwhelming desire to lift her off her feet, lay her on the bed, and wrap her against him and kiss her.

Even now, the image of her half-lidded eyes upon him sent another spear of desire through him. He'd had a difficult time over the past week resisting his longing for her, especially because it had been so strong since lying with her in bed. It was almost as if those kisses had awakened him, and now his needs were clamoring to be fed.

However, he couldn't feed them. He had to give Clarabelle the time she needed to reconcile with her sister. Apparently the efforts weren't having any success, and he was tempted to ride over to High C Ranch and lecture Clementine for being selfish and difficult over all that had happened.

Yet every time he started to saddle the mare, he had only to think of how he'd treated Eric, just how selfish and difficult he'd been. What right did he have to go over and berate Clementine for her behavior when his had been so much worse?

The truth was, even if he talked to Clementine and made it clear that his intentions had ever and only been for Clarabelle, it wouldn't change the fact that Clarabelle hadn't chosen him. She'd pushed him away. And until she was ready for him, she'd probably keep pushing him away.

Ahead of him, Mr. Bliss finished ascending the gradually rising hill, and at the top he halted and pushed up the brim of his Stetson. "I think this is it." His attention went back and forth between the map and the area ahead of him.

Franz scrambled up the last of the incline, then drew a breath into his burning lungs and surveyed the area ahead. The faint light of dawn outlined more rocks looming along the eastern skyline. Although Franz couldn't see the waterfall amidst those rocks, he could hear the rushing sound of it.

Mr. Bliss scaled a boulder. "Just over there."

Franz climbed after him, going much more slowly and carefully. He tried to imagine Eric carrying a safe out to this location in an effort to protect his valuables. It probably hadn't been an easy feat.

The rushing of the waterfall grew louder until at last he stepped beside Mr. Bliss at the edge, the water cascading down a short cliff and flowing into the stream that they'd followed up the mountainside.

Eric's letter had indicated that the safe was in a cavern at the base of the waterfall, so they were close.

Mr. Bliss held up his lantern behind the spray of the water. He surveyed the area, then locked in on something. "Found it."

He handed off the lantern to Franz while he poured gunpowder into the keyhole on the safe. He lit it and ducked away from the waterfall. A moment later, an explosion resounded off the rocky cliffs.

The cavern and the waterfall helped to diminish the sound to some degree, but it still echoed in the silence of the early morning, causing worry to tighten Franz's gut at the prospect that anyone in the area who'd been keeping an eye on the farm might have heard the detonation.

Would they follow and search for him and Mr. Bliss? Or would they go to the cabin first and threaten Clarabelle and the children to gain information?

Mr. Bliss made quick work of tossing Franz the contents from within the safe. Two leather pouches. From the clink and shape of the first one, Franz guessed it contained the remainder of the gold and silver coins Eric had brought with him to America. Even though the amount had only been a small portion of the wealth that belonged to their family, it had still been significant enough that Eric had been able to afford anything he'd wanted.

From the heaviness of the pouch, Franz guessed Eric hadn't wanted to dip too far into his supply. He'd likely wanted to save it for Luisa to use if anything ever happened to him. Or maybe he'd hoped to give it to Dieter and Bianca someday. Perhaps Eric had also wanted Clarabelle to have it in order to be able to take care of the children.

The other leather pouch was smaller. As Franz untied the thong and pried the bag open, he found several rings, a gold hair pin, a ruby brooch, earrings, and a silver pocket watch that had once belonged to their father. None of the jewelry was of any great monetary value. Eric had probably locked them away more for sentimental reasons, so that, again, he could someday pass them along to his children.

Mr. Bliss climbed out from behind the waterfall and was holding another envelope. "This has to be it."

Franz hoped so. He wanted to put an end to the danger that seemed to be constantly lurking since Eric's death.

Mr. Bliss slit open the envelope, drew out a folded paper, then began to read silently. When he finished, he lifted somber eyes to Franz. "It's not good news."

Franz's pulse quieted to a patter. "What do you mean?"

"Seems as though your brother was coerced into becoming a passer."

"What is a passer?"

"The printer rarely passes the money himself. Almost always has a network of passers he uses—men who take the counterfeit money to pass along as real."

Franz shook his head. "Eric would never get involved in something like that—"

"He had no choice." Mr. Bliss handed Franz the letter.

Franz put on his spectacles, leaned into the lantern light, and read it. The note wasn't long, but with each word his heart sank a little lower.

Eric explained that after poor crops, he'd needed to exchange several of his Deutsche Marks to American currency. As he'd done in the past, he'd taken his coins to the assayer to have them tested in order to have the proof of their quality of gold when he exchanged them at the bank.

The new assayer in town, Mr. Grover, had offered to mint them and turn them into American gold coins. Not only had the man minted the coins Eric needed, but he'd also provided bank notes in exchange for some of the gold.

Eric had used most of the American money without any trouble, but then, while in Denver last autumn, one of the bank notes had been identified as fraudulent. With a little investigating, Eric had learned that counterfeit moneymaking was a big problem, and that often the printers lived in remote places, sometimes in little towns in the mountains. He'd also learned that minting coins was illegal, that only official US Mints could make coins.

When Eric had returned to Breckenridge, he'd gone back to the assayer's office and confronted Mr. Grover about the fake money and the illegally minted coins. The assayer had denied any wrongdoing, even when Eric had threatened to report him to the local lawman. But going to the sheriff had been a naïve and dangerous tactic.

Franz wasn't surprised to discover that the sheriff had sided with Mr. Grover. Not long after the incident, Eric had been given an ultimatum—keep quiet and become a passer, or face repercussions not only for himself but also for his family.

He'd felt he had no choice except to do what they'd

asked of him. He'd finally reached out to the Pinkerton Agency in the spring.

But clearly, the help hadn't come soon enough. There was no doubt in Franz's mind that Eric had been murdered because he'd tried to expose the counterfeiting operation. Or perhaps because he'd wanted to get out of it.

Franz finished reading Eric's letter. "So, Mr. Grover is the one behind everything."

"We don't know if he's in charge of the operation." Mr. Bliss surveyed the surrounding area as though making sure they were still alone. "But as an assayer, he would certainly know how to make coins that used other elements in place of some of the gold. And he would likely have the chemicals and other ingredients available for the printing of fake money."

"His wife is the schoolteacher. Clarabelle had nothing but positive things to say about her."

"It's possible she doesn't know about her husband's illegal activities."

It was also possible Mrs. Grover had known and had no choice but to turn a blind eye. According to Clarabelle, the woman was always doing good for the community she lived in. Maybe she did so out of guilt or with the hope of making up for the damage her husband was causing.

Mr. Bliss glanced at the ever-lightening sky.

"Hopefully I'll find the equipment in the shed behind his office and the fake currencies where Eric said they're hidden."

"And hopefully, with Eric's written testimony, you will have enough to convict him."

Mr. Bliss's expression was still serious. "Even if I'm able to arrest the assayer before he runs off, you and your family will remain in danger."

"We will?"

"If Eric was coerced into it, there's no telling how many other people are a part of the operation. Could be a dozen or more men working together."

"Can we discover who else?"

"Eventually it's possible the authorities can get Mr. Grover to release the names of his accomplices. Even then we might not know everyone, might not find out who killed your brother."

"But why would anyone hurt me or Clarabelle? We were not involved in anything."

"Once I raid the assayer's office and attempt to catch Mr. Grover, they'll assume you're the one responsible for contacting me and bringing me up to Breckenridge. And they'll be sure to let you know they're not happy about your interference."

"I will tell them that Eric was the one who contacted you."

Mr. Bliss scoffed. "These are dangerous people, Mr.

Meyer. I don't need to remind you that what happened to your brother could happen again."

What would they do next? Franz's mind reeled with the possibilities. He didn't even want to think about someone coming out to the farm again. Eric's death and the plundering of the cabin had been more than sweet little Bianca could bear. How would she survive if anything else happened?

And what if the attackers did something to hurt Clarabelle or the children as a way to send him a message to stay out of their business? If they'd threatened to harm Eric's children once in order to get him to comply, then what would stop them this time?

His blood turned icy just thinking about the peril.

Mr. Bliss took the letter back from Franz and began to fold it up. "I can tell that you love your wife and your brother's children more than anything. So if I were you, I'd do whatever I had to in order to keep them safe."

Mr. Bliss was right. Franz did love Clarabelle and the children more than anything, and he had to find a way to protect them. "What do you suggest?"

"I'd pack up and leave on the next stagecoach. Go back to Germany and take them with you."

"I cannot do that." He'd told Mr. Bliss earlier in the night about his life in Germany and that he planned to return. But how could he explain that he couldn't take Clarabelle with him—at least at the moment? Clarabelle didn't want to have anything to do with a relationship after all that had happened with Clementine. Even when she hadn't been in the process of pushing him away, he hadn't wanted to ask her to leave her life behind. As much as he longed to be with her, he had yet to figure out how that would work, and he needed more time to do so.

Mr. Bliss slipped Eric's letter back in the envelope. "That probably isn't the news you wanted to hear. But I know what it's like from personal experience to have someone you love hurt by a criminal." His voice dropped low. "If I'd had a way out of the danger, I would have taken it."

Franz's thoughts raced. He had to do something, but what? Was leaving really the best option? "Could we travel to Denver for a few weeks? Would that suffice?" But even as he asked the question, he already knew the answer. The threat would likely linger for a long time. Maybe it wouldn't ever go away.

He had no choice but to take Clarabelle and the children away, and the best place was halfway around the world in Germany, where they would be far from all the problems. The truth was, he could give them a good life there. He could open up the family estate in Neubrandenburg, and they could live there for part of the year. He could also buy—or build—a home in Berlin, where they would be able to live while the university was in session.

The trouble was that he didn't think he could leave Colorado or America if Clarabelle refused to come with him. And the last thing he wanted to do was coerce her into being with him. He'd already resolved that he wanted her to be willing.

What could he do to get her to change her mind about him and be agreeable to leaving on the stagecoach in a few hours?

He didn't know. But he had to figure something out.

20

"That means we have to leave." Franz's pronouncement echoed through the cabin, the tension in each word reverberating through Clarabelle.

She stood in front of the stove, where she'd been cooking breakfast when Franz had returned a short while ago. Dieter and Bianca sat side by side on the sofa, both still in their night clothes, the early morning light beginning to brighten the room and showing the surprise on their young faces at Franz's statement.

Mr. Bliss hadn't come inside—had apparently wanted to be on his way before anyone spotted him on the premises. And now Franz had just finished explaining the trip up into Elk Gulch—how they'd located the safe and the pouches of valuables as well as the letter from Eric that had been inside.

Franz had also told them about the counterfeit moneymaking operation Eric had discovered and tried to stop. Clarabelle guessed that was why Eric had been murdered—because he'd opposed the crime, and someone had wanted to silence him.

"We need to go today," Franz said again emphatically. He'd taken off his hat but still remained by the door as if he had every intention of walking right back outside and riding away in the next instant.

Dieter's eyes were wide upon Franz. "Where are we going, Uncle Franz?"

"To Germany."

"You want us to move to Germany?" Bianca hopped to her knees on the sofa.

"Yes. I would like you to come back with me to Germany." Franz was answering Bianca, but he was looking directly at Clarabelle. "There we will be very far from all the danger."

Bianca clapped. "Yes! I want to move away from the danger."

Dieter scooted to the edge of the sofa. "Will we live with you, Uncle Franz?"

"Of course. I have a castle on the lake where we will stay until I am able to find a suitable home in Berlin for us."

"A castle?" Bianca jumped off the sofa and clapped again. "I'd like to live in a castle."

"On the lake?" This time Dieter's voice rose with excitement. No doubt he was picturing all the fun he could have living by the water.

Clarabelle pressed a hand against her chest as if that could stop the swell of surprise. Franz had told her about his family having a home on a lake, but he hadn't explained it was a castle. She supposed it made sense that, as a wealthy nobleman, he would have a large home. But a castle?

"What do you think, Clarabelle?" he asked hesitantly. "Would you be willing to come with us?"

"You'll come with us, won't you?" Bianca smiled expectantly. "Who else will be my Mutti?"

"You're married to Franz." Dieter's expression was earnest. "That means we need you to stay with him."

Franz didn't add anything, but he was watching her with just as much anticipation. Had he purposefully brought up the move around the children so that he'd have their help to convince her?

But how could she make such a life-altering decision so quickly? Surely Franz didn't expect her to make up her mind now.

"Please, Clarabelle?" Bianca's sweet voice contained such hope.

Dieter's and Franz's eyes were brimming with hope too.

Saying no was nearly impossible for her already, but this was even harder. Yet she couldn't say yes. She couldn't walk away from Clementine with the unresolved strife between them. If she did, their situation really would be just like Franz and Eric's.

Besides, Germany? How could she move so far away? If she did, would she ever see her family again?

Then there was the issue of herself and Franz. She couldn't deny she cared about him. And everyone in town believed she'd ended up married to him. Even Maverick had finally heard the rumors and had questioned her yesterday when she was at the ranch. Of course, she'd explained the truth to him. But the fact remained that she and Franz didn't have an official marriage, which meant she couldn't simply leave with him for Germany.

The scent of burning bacon began to waft in the air. She grabbed the towel and pushed the skillet off the heat and toward the back of the stove where the pan of scrambled eggs was staying warm.

"Please, please, please, Clarabelle?" Bianca's eyes turned glassy.

Tears began to form in Clarabelle's eyes.

The three didn't move or speak as they waited for her answer.

With another swell of pressure rising in her chest, Clarabelle backed away from the stove. She had to get out of the room before she broke down and cried in front of everyone.

Rapidly, she crossed the room, sidled past Franz, and exited the cabin. As soon as she closed the door behind her, the tears spilled over and rolled down her cheeks. She started across the yard toward the barn, her chest aching more than she could bear.

She didn't know what to do or where to go. And somehow she ended up in the stall with her mare. Clarabelle buried her face against the creature's neck and dug her hands in the mane. The soft hair absorbed her tears, and the warm body bore her weight.

The mare gave a nicker as if to offer her a word of comfort.

She patted the horse, grateful to the simple creature for her unwavering support and strength. She'd loved growing up on a ranch in Colorado. She loved the horses. She loved the wildness of the land. And even now on Eric's farm, she loved the work, the simplicity, and the beauty. How could she ever trade her life here for any place else?

"Clarabelle?" Franz spoke softly from the stall behind her.

She hadn't heard him come in, and she swiped her damp cheeks.

"I am sorry." His voice held contrition.

There was nothing for him to be sorry about. "You didn't do anything."

"I used the children to pressure you."

With her cheek still resting against the horse, she shrugged. "It's all right."

"No, it was a cowardly way to go about asking you to come along. I suspected you would not be willing to move to Germany for my sake, but I had hoped you might want to do so to remain with the children."

He wasn't entirely right about her willingness to move to Germany for his sake. She couldn't imagine letting him walk out of her life and never seeing him again. But she couldn't tell him that. "I do want to be with the children. I've grown to love them."

"And they you." He paused. "Nevertheless, I should have spoken with you privately first rather than attempting to convince you to go for their sake. It was selfish of me, and I apologize."

She released her grasp of her mare's mane and pivoted to face Franz.

Though the barn was mostly shadowed, the morning light streaming in from a high open window illuminated the interior enough that she could see Franz's face. His forehead was furrowed and his eyes sad with dark circles underneath. He hadn't shaved, and a layer of stubble had formed, making him more handsome—if that were possible.

"I am taking Mr. Bliss's suggestion to leave the area this morning." Franz's expression held resignation. "Once he makes an arrest—if he is able to do so—I want to keep you and the children from any repercussions."

"I understand." She wanted the children to be safe

too. "It's a good idea to take them to Germany, where they can hopefully put the difficult memories of all that has happened behind them."

Franz nodded, then hung his head.

"It truly is for the best, Franz."

He released a long sigh. When he glanced up, his face was lined with anguish. "I want you to come with us, too, Clarabelle."

She could admit that a place deep inside was relieved that he didn't want to leave her behind. Even so, she couldn't agree to going with him, could she?

"I do not think I can leave you behind." His voice turned hoarse.

The ache inside her swelled again and this time hurt even more.

"As Gott is my witness," he whispered, "I love you as I have no other and want to spend the rest of my earthly life showing you my love."

The words penetrated past the barriers she'd been trying to erect. They were hot, burning a trail through her so that she wanted to do nothing more than cross to him and throw herself in his arms.

But she couldn't. If she did, she'd never be able to tell him no. And already, she wasn't sure that she'd have the strength or willpower to do so. Because the truth was, even with all that had happened with Clementine— maybe even because of it—she cared about Franz as she had no other too.

"As much as I want you to be my wife," he continued, "I only want you if you are willing—not out of obligation or duty, and especially not because you cannot, in your kindness, find a way to say no."

The tears sprang to her eyes again. In such a short time of being together, how was it possible he already knew her better than anyone else? He realized just how hard it would be for her to turn down the children's pleas or his confessions.

He held on to one of the stall posts, his grip tight. He was silent for a moment, then he peered away from her, as if bracing himself. "Of course I desperately want you to come with us. But I suspect you will be out of harm's way if you stay with your family. No one would dare touch you if you go back home."

She certainly wasn't a threat to anyone in the counterfeit operation, was she?

"If you don't want to go, then say no."

Had she ever told anyone no before in her life? How could she start now?

"I want you to have the freedom with me to say no." His face held quiet resignation. "If you tell me no, I will not be angry. And I will not try to make you change your mind."

"Thank you." Her throat was tight, but she managed to squeeze the words out.

"So? What will you say? Yes or no?"

She knew what she had to do. But even as she opened her mouth, she couldn't answer him.

"Say it, Clarabelle"—his whisper echoed with pain— "and I will go away and not bother you again."

She sucked a breath into her burning lungs. She didn't know how she could endure telling him no, but there were too many reasons why she couldn't say yes. She had to do it. He was making this so easy for her, more than anyone else ever had. If she didn't learn how to say no now, how would she ever?

"No." The word came out barely a whisper.

But from the way he bowed his head, as though in defeat, she knew he'd heard.

She'd done it. She'd finally told someone no. But she'd most definitely hurt him in her denial, and she hated knowing that.

Maybe she'd made a mistake. Should she tell him yes instead? She opened her mouth to say more—to tell him she was sorry, to offer any solution that would make him happy.

As soon as the words of excuse formed, she clamped her lips closed. She couldn't leave with Clementine so angry with her. It wouldn't be right. She loved her sister too much to abandon her for a man—even a wonderful man like Franz.

Even though it might be the hardest thing she'd ever

done, she had to let him go.

Franz stood with his head down. Finally, he straightened and drew in a deep breath, as though bracing himself for what he needed to do. "Would you be willing to ride home to your family's ranch? Just until we are gone?"

She nodded and brushed her hand over her mare, unable to get any words past the lump in her throat.

His beautiful blue eyes brimmed with sadness. "It will be easier on everyone not to say goodbye."

No goodbye? She couldn't imagine not hugging and kissing the children one last time. But perhaps Franz was right. If the children pleaded with her again to come with them, would she be able to say no to them?

She'd been able to speak the word to Franz, but she wasn't sure if she could do it again this morning, especially if they started crying.

She nodded.

With a final long look, Franz took her in as though memorizing her features. Then he released the post and walked away. He didn't look back, even though she wanted him to—even when he disappeared through the barn doors.

21

Franz's heart wrenched into more broken pieces as the wagon rolled farther from the farm. The children sat mutely in the wagon bed. Neither had spoken a word since they'd left.

He'd hardly been able to utter anything either since he'd walked out of the barn and away from Clarabelle.

But he'd forced one foot in front of the other until he'd reached the cabin. When he'd stepped inside, he'd closed the door and wrestled against the overwhelming urge to fling it open and race back to her.

The children had been sitting at the table, eating their breakfast and blissfully unaware of the turmoil that had been gathering. They'd been chattering happily about the prospects that awaited them in Germany and had peppered him with questions about their new home and life.

He'd answered as best he could as he'd leaned against

the door. And when he'd finally heard Clarabelle passing down the lane on her horse, he'd gripped the door handle until his fingers had ached.

Finally, when he could hold himself back no longer, he'd stepped outside to shout at her, to beg her not to leave, to plead with her to go with them, but she was already halfway down the lane.

Thankfully, she hadn't looked back. Because if she had, he probably wouldn't have stopped himself from running after her. As it was, he'd only stood mutely on the stoop, until the children had joined him, still excited and still unaware that Clarabelle wouldn't be their Mutti any longer.

He'd gathered the courage to tell them only after he'd loaded the trunk with their belongings into the back of the wagon and helped them up beside it. Only then had he let them know that Clarabelle was already gone, and he'd given them no time to protest—had instead climbed onto the wagon bench and started toward town.

During the silent ride, he'd composed a letter in his mind to Clarabelle, reiterating his love for her, letting her know she would always be a part of him, that he'd never love another woman again.

He also wanted to ask her not to live on Eric's farm by herself. Even if the counterfeiters might not specifically target her, he would feel better if she returned to her family's ranch and sold Eric's place. He couldn't even think of the possibility that she would find someone else to marry, someone who would be willing to stay there and help her manage it.

Just the prospect sent his thoughts into a dark tunnel that he knew he couldn't venture down—not now that the children were his priority and his sole responsibility.

As he directed the wagon down the grassy path toward the cemetery, he tried to rein in his despondency. After the children had lost their father and mother and sister, the loss of Clarabelle would likely be another difficult adjustment. He had to stay strong for them, even though he wanted to shout and scream at the unfairness of everything.

He'd come this far and found Clarabelle, a treasure beyond anything he could have imagined. Now the idea of riding out of town on the stagecoach without her made him almost physically sick.

"Gott in heaven above," he whispered, "have mercy on my poor soul." If there was any way to be together with Clarabelle, he needed to find it.

As he brought the wagon to a halt in front of the cemetery gate, he pressed a hand to his aching heart.

"What are we doing here, Uncle Franz?" Dieter had risen and was peering at the graveyard.

"We've come to say goodbye to your parents." Even though they didn't have much time before the stagecoach left town, Franz needed to stop, not only for himself but for the children. This might be the last time they would ever be able to do this.

Mr. Bliss was planning to arrest Mr. Grover but had agreed to wait until they were gone on the stagecoach. He'd said that he couldn't delay another day; it would be too risky. He couldn't chance Mr. Grover or anyone else seeing him and having the time to escape or hide the presses and other tools.

The element of surprise was vitally important. In fact, Mr. Bliss had indicated even Franz's leaving town with his family could raise suspicions and put the counterfeiters on alert. Mr. Bliss had warned Franz to be extra watchful, even on the stagecoach—that he probably wouldn't be truly safe until he was well out of Colorado.

Franz helped the children out of the wagon and together they entered the cemetery. As he passed by the headstones with Clarabelle's parents' names, he paused. The area was clean, the weeds pulled, a handful of wilted flowers on the freshly dug gravesite—probably from Clarabelle.

She stopped by from time to time to try to connect with her mother in some small way. Maybe that was another reason she'd never want to leave America— because she had too many ties to the place and the land. He couldn't blame her and wasn't angry at her for choosing her life here over a life with him. But it still hurt.

He could only pray she would find happiness and peace. That's all he truly wanted for her.

With a sigh, he moved on and followed the children to the section where their family was buried. Three gravestones marked the spots for Eric, Luisa, and their little sister Amalie. Franz reached for Dieter's and Bianca's hands, and together they stood side by side.

Eric's last words echoed through Franz's mind. *"I never meant to fall in love with her. I tried not to. But now she is my life and all that matters to me. I know that is difficult to understand, but I pray someday you will."*

At the time, Franz had thought Eric was giving him another excuse to justify stealing Luisa from him. After meeting Clarabelle, he could finally understand the love Eric had had for Luisa.

Yes, the two had been wrong in how they'd gone about things. Eric should have come to him and told him before pursuing her. Luisa should have put an end to one relationship before starting another.

But it was past time for him to acknowledge their relationship itself hadn't been wrong. Perhaps the two had even been perfect for each other. If Eric had felt for Luisa even a fraction of what he felt for Clarabelle, then they probably had been meant to be together.

"I'm sorry, Eric." He whispered the words. It was also past time for him to ask Eric to forgive him.

The children were looking up at him, likely

wondering what he was apologizing for. Maybe someday he'd be able to tell them all that had happened. Or maybe it was best if that part of the past was left behind here in America. The tragedy, the heartache, the scandal could forever be buried with Eric and Luisa and wouldn't need to taint the children's memory of their parents.

He just prayed that Eric could somehow hear his plea for forgiveness.

Regardless, Franz had to do as Clarabelle had suggested. He had to ask God to forgive him, and he had to finally forgive himself. Now that he'd come to the end of his journey in Colorado and America, he couldn't leave until he'd done so.

He lowered himself to one knee and bowed his head.

From the corner of his eyes, he could see the children following his example, and the sight of them on one knee with their heads bowed brought him fresh resolve to live with integrity.

He closed his eyes and prayed for forgiveness, a clean soul, and that he could be a worthy father figure to the children. Most of all he prayed that someday God would find a way to reunite him with the woman he loved.

22

Trying to find solace, Clarabelle brushed a hand across the velvety flank of the newest foal—one that was just two days old.

When Hazel had greeted Clarabelle warmly upon her arrival a short while ago, she'd taken one look at Clarabelle's tear-streaked face, hugged her, and then told her she had just the thing to cheer her up.

The sight of the spindly-legged filly had indeed cheered Clarabelle . . . for a few minutes. But as soon as Hazel had gone off to check on another of the broodmares who was expecting, Clarabelle's tears had started again.

The paddock attached to the mare barn contained several mare and foal pairs. They were all grazing peacefully in the bright morning sunshine.

If only she could have just a tiny bit of their peace for her soul. But since riding away from Franz and the children, her soul had felt like it was being tormented.

In her heart, she was convinced she'd done the right thing in leaving Franz so that she could protect her relationship with Clementine. Considering how hurt Clementine still was, Clarabelle could only imagine the damage that running off with Franz would have caused. Clementine probably wouldn't have spoken to her ever again.

Clarabelle ran her hand over the filly's crest and then her withers. The human touch was important at this early age, and normally Clarabelle loved helping with the task of taming the foals.

But today she kept glancing at the house, waiting for Clementine to come out and saddle up her horse to ride into town. Clarabelle wanted to try to talk again. Maybe it would help if she shared that Franz was leaving and that she'd turned down his offer to go with him.

Clarabelle shook her head. Clementine would probably accuse her of gloating.

And what about Franz and the children? They were likely already on their way to town, if not already on the stagecoach. The very thought of the miles that separated them sent a strange desperation careening through Clarabelle.

What was she doing letting them go away without her? What if she never saw them again?

More tears rolled down her cheeks.

"Oh, for heaven's sake." She'd cried more over Franz in the past day than she'd ever cried before in her entire life.

"Wanna tell me what's going on?" came a man's voice nearby.

Clarabelle startled and rubbed her sleeve across the wetness on her cheeks.

It was Maverick, and he was in the open barn door only a dozen paces away, leaning casually against the wooden frame, watching her, and obviously had been long before she'd realized he was there.

"I'm fine." She forced cheerfulness into her voice. "A little tired this morning, that's all."

"That ain't all, darlin'." With his muscular arms folded across his rugged frame, Maverick didn't move from his spot. "C'mon now. Tell me what's wrong."

She had no doubt Hazel had gone straight to Maverick and told him something was wrong with her. Now, as her big brother, he probably felt it was his duty to fix her problems like he usually did. But this was one problem he couldn't fix.

"The big question is why you're here this morning and not over at your own place." Maverick's sun-browned face was wreathed with concern lines. "Not that I don't like seeing you here, but don't the children need you there?"

She hadn't told anyone yet why she was at the ranch.

First, she didn't want to say too much about the counterfeiting operation until Mr. Bliss had the chance to accomplish his mission.

Second, she wasn't sure she wanted to admit she'd lost everything when she'd said one tiny word earlier. She'd not only lost Franz but also given up the children and essentially the farm too. Because she didn't want to live there without Franz or the children.

The longer she stalled, the deeper Maverick's frown grew, until at last he pushed away from the door and began to stalk toward her. "Reckon you best tell me everything without holding back."

"Oh, Maverick. I made a mess of things."

He halted beside her. "Are you talking about the bickering between you and Clem?"

She nodded. She supposed everyone on the ranch knew Clementine was mad at her.

"C'mon. I have a feeling this is a long story." He guided her to the paddock fence, and they climbed up and sat side by side as they'd done many times in the past.

Maverick had always been easy to talk to, and she knew she could trust him with the whole truth about everything that had transpired over recent days. She started by telling him how she and Clementine had both fallen for Franz and that Clementine was upset because she'd been dishonest about her feelings for Franz.

Then she shared about the Pinkerton agent arriving

last night and the information Franz and Mr. Bliss had uncovered in Eric's safe. She told Maverick all about the counterfeit money operation and how Eric had gotten involved in it against his will. She explained how Eric had tried to stop it and that, hopefully, the information he'd left in the safe would prove useful to Mr. Bliss.

"That's a lot to take in." Maverick had hooked his boot heels on one of the fence rungs and was leaning forward, bracing his elbows on his knees. "But seems like the situation between you and Clem is pretty cut and dried."

"How so?"

"Reckon anyone who's ever seen Franz around you can tell he's got Cupid's cramp something awful."

Franz's last words to her had been filtering through her mind since she'd left him. *I love you as I have no other and want to spend the rest of my earthly life showing you my love.*

Maverick was peering at her sideways. "He told you he loved you, didn't he?"

What harm could come from admitting it now? "Yes."

"And you love him back." It wasn't a question.

She hesitated. Was there any doubt that she loved Franz in return? After the misery she'd felt since leaving him, how could she keep denying her love? "I do love him, Maverick. More than anyone or anything." More than her family, more than her dreams of becoming a teacher, more than the ranch where she'd grown up, more than even Dieter and Bianca.

Maverick grinned and sat up. "Then what exactly is the problem here? If you love him, then go back home and tell him that."

"I can't. Clementine is still upset with me, and I don't want to ruin our relationship over our disagreement about a man."

Maverick bumped up the brim of his hat so that the full force of his blue eyes was upon her. "Someone very wise once told me that friendship is a gift and I should be a good friend, but the person I love needs to take priority over anyone else."

Clarabelle couldn't hold back a smile in return. She'd told Maverick that very thing when he'd had relationship trouble with Hazel earlier in the spring.

"Can you honestly tell me," Maverick continued, "that you're willing to give up the one you love because you don't want to upset Clem?"

Again, Maverick was turning her advice around and pointing it right at her. And coming from him, her excuses for not staying with Franz sounded silly. Was that what she was doing, rejecting Franz's love so that she didn't hurt Clementine's feelings?

"You know Clementine." Maverick had turned his gaze to Clementine, who was now exiting the house. Even hatless, with her hair in disarray and with a shawl hanging half off her shoulder, she radiated life and beauty like no one else. "She'll be upset for a week or two, but then she'll get over whatever it is and forget all about it."

"We've never fought like this before, though."

"That's because you always give in to her. And this time you didn't. You hung on to Franz."

"I guess I did." Wordlessly, she had told Clementine no, that she couldn't have Franz.

"Now that you hung on to what you wanted, she's pouting that she didn't get her way for once."

"It's more than pouting."

"By giving in to her being upset, you're just teaching her that she can pout and get what she wants after all."

Was that true?

He nodded as if to confirm it. "This is one time when you need to stop worrying about what she thinks. She'll eventually adjust and realize she can't always have her way."

Clementine began to walk toward the barn, swinging a basket by her side—probably filled with candy to refill her supplies at the store. She lifted her face to the sun, letting the rays add more freckles to her face. A pretty smile curved her lips up.

Was her brother right? Would Clementine soon forget all about the fight? But what if she didn't? What if she held on to a grudge like Franz had done with Eric for all those years?

Clarabelle wasn't sure she could live with that. But what was worse? Living without Clementine, or living without Franz?

Maybe it was time that she took to heart her own counsel and made Franz a priority over everyone else, even over Clementine. Because the fact was, she loved Franz, and the thought of life without him in it was becoming more depressing with every passing moment.

He was everything she'd ever wanted in a man. Everything. He was passionate and romantic. And he treated her so well, so tenderly, so sweetly all the time. She wanted to be with him and talk to him and share life with him. No one else would ever compare to him.

He was the kind of man a woman met once in a lifetime, and if she let him go now, she'd lose the best thing that had ever happened to her.

With an urgency rising swiftly inside, she jumped down from the fence post. "I have to go after him."

"Thatagirl." Maverick's brows rose in question. "Where is he going?"

"Mr. Bliss told him he'd be safest to return to Germany."

Maverick's smile completely faded as the words sank in. "He wants to take you back with him to Germany?"

She nodded, suddenly anxious to go inside and pack her bag and race after Franz. Did she still have time to make it to town before the stagecoach left?

"Move to Germany?" Maverick's tone turned suddenly hard. "There's no need to be drastic about things. We'll make sure you're safe here."

A dozen excuses floated to the tip of Clarabelle's tongue—all the usual tactics she'd ever used to placate and not upset anyone. But she knew, as she'd done with Franz, that she had to get better at saying just one word.

She swallowed all her trepidation and all her excuses. And she pushed out the word. "No."

Maverick paused in rattling off the ways that he and the other neighbors could ensure their safety, and he stared at her, his mouth open.

Clearly, he wasn't used to hearing her use that word either.

"No." She said it louder this time and more firmly. "If Franz will still have me, I'm going to live in Germany with him."

Maverick's objections flashed in his eyes. Germany was too far away. She hadn't known Franz that long. She was still so young.

Ultimately, none of it mattered. Not when she'd found the person who was made just for her, a perfect fit.

"I need to go pack." She began to cross the paddock toward the barn door. "And then I have a stagecoach to catch."

23

What did a woman moving across the ocean bring with her when she would likely never return?

Clarabelle stuffed the last of her clothing and shoes into the largest canvas bag she'd been able to unearth among her ma's old belongings. She'd also included several of her favorite books, a few mementos and pictures of her family, and some items that had belonged to her ma.

She still had important clothing at the farm and some toiletries. That meant she would have to waste time stopping there on her way into town. But it couldn't be helped.

As she hefted the bag and tried to wrangle the strap over her shoulder, the thudding of horse hooves resounded out the open bedroom window. The pounding had an urgency that set her on edge.

What if something had gone wrong with exposing the

counterfeit operation? And what if the crooks had gone after Franz and the children? Maybe one of them had been hurt.

With her heart slamming against her ribs, Clarabelle crossed to the window, pushed the curtains aside, and peered out at the grassy yard that stood between the house and the barns. A single rider on a horse—a tall man with brown hair and a short, trimmed beard, along with broad shoulders and a body that always looked like it had been hewn from rock.

Ryder. Her adopted brother.

His tan Stetson sat low over his face, shadowing him and keeping her from gauging his expression. He carried a bundle in one arm, as if he had an important delivery.

At least she would be able to say goodbye to him before she left Colorado. She wouldn't be able to say farewell to Tanner, her other adopted brother, since only the good Lord knew where in the mountains he was on any given day.

Her bag was heavy and cumbersome, and by the time she made it outside and down the stairs of the raised porch, Ryder had already dismounted and was talking with Maverick near the mare barn. Clementine was in the process of leading her horse out of the other barn, saddled and ready to ride into town.

Clarabelle lowered her bag to the ground, hoping Clementine would at least hug her goodbye. As much as she was resolving to put Franz first, she couldn't fathom parting ways with Clementine if they were still at odds.

Maverick was bending over Ryder's bundle, peeking carefully. As a wail filled the air, Maverick jumped back and threw up his hands as though he wanted nothing to do with the wailing creature.

Was it a puppy or a kitten?

Clementine, obviously seeing the commotion, veered toward the two men. Even though Clarabelle knew she needed to go straight to the barn and retrieve her mare, she made her way toward Ryder too.

"She doesn't want him." Ryder's voice held a note of panic. His brown eyes were almost frantic, and as he locked in on her approach first, then Clementine's, he expelled a breath. "Thank the heavens you're both here. I need your help."

Clarabelle was close enough to see that Ryder held a wiggling bundle . . . a red-faced newborn, who was scrunching up his face as though preparing to release another cry.

"Sadie gave birth to the baby yesterday." Ryder held the child out toward Clarabelle, his expression begging her to take him.

As much as Clarabelle wanted to hold the newborn, she had to go. Every second she delayed meant more of a chance that she'd miss catching the stagecoach.

Clementine shot Clarabelle a look of censure before

taking the baby from Ryder and cradling him in her arm. "Aw, he's adorable, Ryder."

"Sadie doesn't want him. She said I had to take him, or she'll put him in an orphanage." At the mention of the word *orphanage*, Ryder's tone hardened. He didn't have fond memories of his time in orphanages, and no doubt he'd do anything to keep his own son from going there.

"Why doesn't she want to raise the baby?" Maverick was still a couple feet away and watching the baby with wide eyes.

"Who knows with Sadie." Ryder shook his head, the frustration rolling off him as it usually did whenever he talked about his wife—now his ex-wife since she'd run off with Axe Lyman, the owner of Wild Whiskey Saloon, and had gotten a divorce from Ryder.

The whole ordeal had been difficult. Now Sadie was making things even more challenging. With a new ranch to look after, how would Ryder be able to care for a newborn too?

"I'm planning to hire help." Ryder took off his hat and jammed his fingers in his hair, a habit he had whenever he was nervous. "But until I can locate someone, I need you girls to take care of the baby."

Clementine smiled down at the infant. "Of course I'll help. I'll do whatever I can."

Ryder's expectant gaze swung to Clarabelle.

"I'd like to, I really would—"

"Good. Thank you both. I knew I could count on you."

The same panic from earlier began to pulse through Clarabelle. She had to say no. Again. Why was this still so hard?

The desperation in Ryder's eyes was beginning to wane. "I promise, I'll place an ad today or tomorrow."

Clementine tucked the blanket around the infant more firmly. "Maybe it would be best if you look for a wife who could be a mother to this fellow. You could put a notice in one of the matrimonial catalogs."

Ryder arched his brow. "What's wrong with hiring someone?"

"It costs money you don't have." Of course Clementine was as blunt as always.

Clarabelle drew in a breath and willed herself to be equally as fearless. "I can't help you, Ryder. I'm sorry."

Ryder had opened his mouth to reply to Clementine, and now it hung open.

Clarabelle didn't want to cause conflict, hated the idea that she was letting anyone down, wanted to please everyone. But she couldn't. She had to stay strong. "I'm moving to Germany with Franz and the children."

Silence fell over the yard except for the grunting half cries of the baby.

Clementine's eyes filled first with surprise, then hurt. Without saying a word, she started toward the house, the baby still in her arms.

"Wait." Clarabelle reached out a hand as if that could somehow make her sister come back to her. But with a stiff spine, Clementine didn't break her stride.

"I'm leaving today," Clarabelle called, unable to keep the quiver from her voice. "Right now."

Clementine still didn't stop.

"Goodbye, Clem." Clarabelle wanted to tack on another apology, but over the past week, she'd already said she was sorry a dozen times in a dozen different ways. That had to be enough.

Even so, she waited for Clementine's response.

"I love you." Clarabelle spoke the words and prayed her sister would at least turn and look at her one last time. But Clementine paused for only a moment as she reached the door, then she ducked her head and stepped inside, shutting the door behind her.

The ache in Clarabelle's heart swelled painfully.

Maverick laid a gentle hand upon her arm, his eyes radiating compassion. "I'll go get our horses while you say goodbye to Ryder."

"You don't have to come with me."

"I want to see you off." He gave her nose a soft tweak. "It might be a long time until I get to see you again."

Her throat closed up. She knew what he was leaving unsaid—that they might never get to see each other again. Although she wanted to protest more, that she couldn't take him away from his work, she was glad he'd offered to ride with her into town.

She said her goodbyes to Hazel, Ryder, and the few ranch hands who were around. Then she mounted and rode away from her childhood home and everything familiar. As she reached the woods and the bend in the road that would take her home from view, she paused and glanced back for a final time.

Clementine stood at the front window of the house. Clarabelle couldn't see her clearly, didn't really know if she was watching. But she lifted a hand in farewell anyway.

Slowly, Clementine raised a hand too and pressed it against the glass.

Clarabelle's throat ached with a swell of emotion. It wasn't the reconciliation she'd hoped for, but it was something she could carry with her in the days to come.

After stopping by the farm and getting the rest of what she needed, she and Maverick pushed their horses hard into town. Even with the fast pace, Clarabelle was glad for Maverick's company and was relieved when he promised to do what he could to make sure the livestock and produce at the farm were taken care of. It was the least they could do for the memory of Eric and to respect all the work he'd put into creating the farm. Maverick also promised to see if he could find a buyer for the place and insisted that he would send the sale money to her once he knew where she was settled.

Would she ever feel settled in a new place? Not only would she be a world away from everyone she loved, but she'd be a world away from everything that was familiar. She could admit she'd miss the rugged and often hard life in the mountains. She'd miss the breathtaking beauty. She'd even miss the hard work.

In her heart, she'd always consider herself a rancher. But hopefully she'd learn to love her new life too. As long as she had Franz by her side, she'd be satisfied.

As the town came into view, nestled along the Blue River between two mountain ranges, she searched frantically for a sight of the man she loved and wanted to be with for the rest of her life.

But she didn't spot him or the children anywhere, and she didn't see the stagecoach either. Was she too late?

She and Maverick galloped the last of the distance until they reached the livery, where the stagecoach usually departed. Maverick hopped down before she could and was already in the wide-open double doors of the barnlike structure.

"Grady?" he called into the shadows. "The stagecoach leave town?"

"Yep," came a reply. "Left at nine a.m. sharp."

Clarabelle released a huff of frustration. If only she'd come to her senses earlier. Or if only she hadn't pushed Franz away.

"What time is it now?" Maverick didn't carry a watch the way Franz did, since most ranchers told time by the natural rhythms of the livestock and the hours of daylight.

"About half past nine," came Grady's reply.

Maverick trotted back over to the horses and peered up at her. "How badly do you want to be with your man?"

"I can't live without him."

Maverick gave her one of his charming grins. "Then c'mon, darlin'. We've got some work to do."

24

Franz gripped the seat of the stagecoach to keep himself from throwing open the door and making the driver stop.

He hadn't wanted to get on board. He hadn't wanted to leave town. He hadn't wanted to go anywhere except back to Clarabelle.

On the seat on either side of him, Dieter and Bianca were enjoying every moment of the ride, peering out the windows and watching the scenery passing by. The somberness from leaving Clarabelle and from their stop at the cemetery had lessened with the excitement of the new adventure.

If only he could find any joy or excitement at the prospect of what lay ahead. But with every mile that came between him and Clarabelle, his muscles tightened with the need to put a stop to the conveyance.

Not only did he hate leaving her behind, but he also hated that she would have to face the rumors about their relationship by herself. That her good name in the community might possibly be ruined because of him. His only hope was that, with time, people would forget about him and realize Clarabelle was as sweet as always.

He shouldn't have left the burdens to fall on her shoulders, shouldn't have left at all.

But he'd already convinced himself numerous times over the past two hours that he had to let her go, that he could only be with her if she were willing to be with him in return. And although he wanted to go back and try again to convince her to be with him, what good would it do?

She wasn't ready to be his—might never be.

If only he'd had more time to win her heart . . .

He released a long, exasperated sigh, which drew the attention of the older man sitting across from him and reading a newspaper. Another fellow reclined on the opposite bench too, but he'd appeared slightly hungover when stepping up into the coach earlier, and now he was sleeping with his head resting against the side, his mouth open and emitting obnoxious snores.

Franz didn't know how anyone could possibly get a moment of rest with all the jostling. He never had learned how to manage the feat—not during his traveling back home or here in America.

A part of him had been scrambling to find a way that he could stay in Colorado. He'd gone over all the options, but every time he did, he came back to the same conclusion. He had too many responsibilities awaiting him at home, and he couldn't just walk away from everything. At least, not without first managing his financial matters, his homes, and officially resigning from the university.

Then there was the matter of his and the children's safety. By now Mr. Bliss would likely have raided the counterfeit printing press at the back of the assayer's office and hopefully arrested Mr. Grover.

Franz had given Mr. Bliss his home address and asked him to apprise him of how things went. He could only hope that Mr. Bliss would be able to eventually discover who'd murdered Eric and prosecute him. At the very least, he'd asked Mr. Bliss to telegram an update to his hotel in Denver, the place he'd stayed before and planned to stay again.

Even as all the rational reasons for leaving clamored through his mind, his heart demanded that he cast them all aside and return to Clarabelle. She'd become the sole reason he had for waking up in the morning, the sole reason for taking each breath throughout his day, the sole reason for thinking about his future.

Without her . . . what did he have?

Bianca bumped against him as the stagecoach rounded a bend in the winding road up Boreas Pass. She turned and peered up at him, then she slipped her hand into his. "It'll be okay, Uncle Franz."

Clearly, she sensed his distress and was doing her five-year-old best to comfort him. But nothing could ease his heartache.

Even so, he bent and kissed the top of her head. He had the children. They needed him, and he couldn't forget that.

At the sound of shouting from behind the stagecoach, Franz lifted a hand to the hard outline of his revolver underneath his shirt. The older man across from him lowered his newspaper and cast an anxious glance out the window.

Franz knew it would do no good to look out. In fact, it might invite more danger, especially if someone was trying to catch him. Although he'd learned marksmanship as a boy, he'd only ever used guns in hunting, never to shoot another human being.

The shouting behind the stagecoach intensified. And then a gunshot rang out. "Stop the stagecoach!" This time the call was clear.

As the vehicle began to slow, Franz's blood turned cold, and he withdrew his gun.

The children were now plastered against the seat, the smiles gone and replaced with worry. The older man with the newspaper was watching him, too, while the sleeping fellow continued to snore.

The stagecoach finally came to a halt, and Franz

tensed. Something told him that the person was there for him.

"Franz Meyer?" came a man's call from behind.

Yes, he was right. He'd hoped to get far away without any confrontations, but that was apparently not to be his luck.

"Is Franz Meyer there?" The question came again, more forcefully.

Franz shifted forward on the seat and moved toward the door. He couldn't sit inside like a coward. He may as well face whomever it was with courage and determination—perhaps even hand himself over to keep everyone else safe.

He grasped Dieter's shoulder. "If anything happens to me, take Bianca back to Breckenridge and find Clarabelle."

Dieter's face was pale, but he nodded bravely.

Franz shifted toward Bianca. "Stay inside the coach with Dieter and listen to him."

With wide eyes, she nodded.

Then, without another moment of hesitation, Franz swung open the door and stepped out. He kept his gun hidden behind his back, not wanting to draw any gunfire right away. As he steadied himself, he took in the horse and rider behind the stagecoach.

The morning sun slanted into Franz's eyes, making it difficult to see the man, but from first appearances the fellow didn't look threatening, didn't have his guns out. With the brim of his hat pulled low, his face was shadowed. Even so, he looked familiar.

"When you rode out of town," the man said, "you left something behind."

Not only did he look familiar, but his voice sounded familiar too.

Franz squinted through the sunshine to get a better look, then his heartbeat took off at a racing gallop. It was Maverick, Clarabelle's brother. Maybe he had a message from Clarabelle.

"Wanted to get it to you before you got too far," Maverick said.

Franz was desperate for anything from Clarabelle. If she gave him even the smallest sign that she wanted to be with him, he'd move heaven and earth to be with her again at some point. Maybe they could write letters and, when she was ready, he could find a way to bring her to Germany if she was willing to move. If not, maybe by then he could return with the children to Breckenridge.

Franz holstered his gun. "I am obliged and will take anything you have for me."

As Maverick motioned behind him and another horse and rider turned the bend, Franz lost his voice along with every coherent thought except one.

Clarabelle was here.

She was atop her mare in all her beauty and was

peering at him shyly, as if she wasn't sure how he'd react to seeing her.

He could only stare, the longing inside swelling so swiftly and keenly his hands trembled. Why was she here? Had she come to be with him?

A large canvas bag was strapped behind her saddle. Was it what he hoped? A bag filled with her belongings because she wanted to go with him?

He opened his mouth to ask, but then was too afraid that she'd offer some other explanation.

Maverick was wearing a wide grin, as if he was enjoying the surprise immensely. "You left Clarabelle behind."

"Did I?" Franz directed his question to Clarabelle.

She was clutching her reins tightly. "I hope I'm not too late to join you."

Oh, thank Gott in heaven above. She was coming. His relief was so great that he had to grab on to the carriage to keep from buckling.

When his answer wasn't immediately forthcoming, her brow furrowed. "I love you, Franz. And I'm sorry it took me so long to realize it. But the truth is, I need to be with you more than anything else."

He closed his eyes for an instant. Was he dreaming? As he opened his eyes to the sight of her still on her horse, watching him and waiting for his response, he knew of only one way to show her how he felt.

He released the carriage and began to cross to her, his steps firm and determined. When he reached her, he lifted up a hand.

She placed hers in his.

As he closed his fingers around hers, the familiar charge of energy crackled in the air. His body, his life blood, his entire being was as magnetically drawn to her now as he'd been when he first met her. Although he wanted to scientifically dissect what was happening to him, he knew the ways of love could never truly be explained. All he did know was that he needed her, that they belonged together, and that his life wouldn't be complete without her.

A small smile began to curve up her lips, as if she could feel their undeniable connection too.

He tugged at her, and in the next instant she was sliding eagerly down. He didn't let her feet touch the ground before he pulled her into his arms and against his body. Her arms wound around his neck and locked there tightly, as if she was afraid to let go of him.

She needn't worry. Because he wasn't planning to release her again. Now that he had her, he wouldn't be able to take his hands off her.

He lowered his mouth to hers to find that she was ready for him. As her lips came against his, there was a fervor in her kiss and in the way she held him that told him she'd been afraid she'd lost him too and that she couldn't bear to live without him.

With each stroke of his mouth against hers, he tried to convey that he loved her and couldn't live without her either. She was his. She was his future. She was his everything.

Maverick's chuckling penetrated Franz's consciousness, and he pulled back, knowing he needed to use restraint or he'd utterly embarrass them both with his passion.

Yet, even though he was no longer kissing her, he couldn't make himself release her. He held her tightly, and she clung to him, her face buried against his chest.

Maverick had gotten down from his mount and was untying Clarabelle's bag from the back of her mare. "Reckon the two of you oughta head straight to a church once you reach Denver. Make your marriage official as soon as possible."

"I like that plan." Franz pressed a kiss to Clarabelle's temple. "What do you think, mein Liebchen? Are you willing to wed me?"

"Oh yes. I'm willing." Her voice was breathless. "Are you?"

"I've been ready to wed you since the day I first met you."

She gazed up at him with her bright green eyes—eyes he could look into forever. And her smile told him she wanted nothing more than to be with him forever too. It was all he could ask for and more.

"Then let's go," he whispered, his voice husky with all the emotion he felt for her.

She nodded. "But first?"

"What?"

"This." She rose on her toes and kissed him again—a kiss that made it very clear that she was indeed willing.

25

As Franz closed their hotel room door, Clarabelle shivered with anticipation—and with amazement at the sheer splendor and luxury of the Grand Palace Hotel in Denver.

They'd done as Maverick had suggested, and after arriving in Denver that afternoon, they'd located the church closest to the stagecoach station and had gotten married in a short ceremony with the children as their witnesses, this time officially.

Afterward, Franz had taken them to an elegant dinner, then they'd come to the hotel. As they'd arrived at the sprawling hotel that took up most of the block, she'd told Franz that they could stay someplace simpler.

But he'd held her hand and tugged her inside, the children following eagerly behind. He'd insisted that he wanted only the very best for his family and his wife. The hotel manager had greeted him warmly and had given him a telegram that Mr. Bliss had sent.

Together, he and Clarabelle had read the telegram, learning that Mr. Bliss had taken Mr. Grover unaware with the raid on the shed behind the assayer's office. Even though Mr. Grover hadn't been making the fake currency at the time, all of the supplies were there, including the stash of false notes that Eric had hidden away to help in the investigation. Mr. Grover had been arrested and had already tried to pin the blame on the sheriff, implicating him in Eric's murder. Apparently the sheriff had denied any part in the counterfeit operation or the murder, but he'd been arrested too.

Franz had been satisfied with the news. Even though nothing was certain and probably wouldn't be until Mr. Grover and the sheriff had trials, at least Eric's death was no longer a mystery.

After exploring the hotel for a short while, she and Franz had tucked the children into bed in the adjoining set of rooms, and Franz had paid extra to have a maid stay with the children through the night.

Clarabelle still couldn't quite get used to the extravagant way Franz spent his money, but he assured her it was nothing. And she guessed it was the lifestyle he was accustomed to—one that was different from anything she'd ever known.

Even now, as she stood at the center of the sitting room, she could only stare with fascination at the elegant mahogany furniture, the settees and matching armchairs positioned in front of the white marble fireplace. Thick blue-green drapes hung in the windows. The wall hangings, rugs, and decorations were all so beautiful that she wasn't sure she should actually touch anything.

A door opened to the bedchamber beyond, revealing a room with an enormous four-poster bed of the same dark mahogany, framed by bedcurtains. A large bouquet of roses graced the bedside table. And the covers on the bed had been turned down to reveal mounds of pillows and silky sheets.

Her body heated just looking at the bed and realizing that she and Franz would be able to share that bed and every bed from now on. They would get to spend each night together and never have to be apart again.

She could admit that ever since those couple of hours they'd lain together in the bed at the farmhouse, she'd been eager for a repeat. She'd wanted to spend hours lying at his side in his arms, with nothing else to do but hold each other and kiss whenever they wanted.

The very idea of doing so seemed bold of her, almost scandalous. But she couldn't deny she wanted him in a way that was deep and visceral.

He finished locking the door and pivoted, taking in the room in one sweeping glance. The satisfied look on his face said it was everything he'd expected. It was also everything he was used to, a world that was far more comfortable for him than the barren and simple cabin at the farm.

He shed his coat and tossed it over the back of the nearest chair. Then he began to unbutton his vest.

Again the temperature in her body began to rise. Watching him taking off his clothing was strangely alluring.

At the last of the buttons, he paused and seemed to realize that she was staring at him, transfixed. Or ogling him.

His gaze roved over her, and his lashes lowered as his nostrils flared. "Have I told you recently that I love you?" His whisper came out softly, reverently.

She laughed lightly. "You told me a minute ago."

He started toward her, his gaze fixed upon her mouth. "It has been too long since I kissed you."

Again she laughed. "That's only been a few minutes too."

"A few minutes too long." He reached for her, grasping both arms and drawing her against his body with an urgent force.

She drew in a sharp breath, her need for him growing urgent too.

He bent in and plundered her mouth with a passion that left her weak. She wanted nothing more than for him to sweep her up off her feet, carry her into the bedroom, and lay her on the bed. She was embarrassed by how much she wanted that.

But instead of sweeping her up, he took a step back and released her.

She almost cried out her protest, and might have if he hadn't lowered himself to one knee before her.

He unbuttoned the top button of his shirt and pulled out the chain that he always wore underneath. He unclasped the chain, then took off the rings that he wore next to his heart at all times.

"I was planning to have a wedding ring made for you—the finest ring in all of Berlin, in all of Germany." He held up an elegant gold ring studded with small diamonds. "But the more I have thought about rings, the more I am convinced that this ring belongs on your finger."

She hesitated. He'd shared how he'd nearly lost his parents' rings on the train after arriving in Denver and how important the rings were in connecting him to his parents. "Are you sure? Your parents' rings are more important to you than anything else."

"*You* are more important than anything else." His voice turned hoarse with emotion. "You are my wife, flesh of my flesh and bone of my bone. We are one. And nothing will ever separate us."

She was always amazed when he talked to her so poetically, passionately, and romantically.

He slipped the ring on her finger. "My parents were

guiding me all this time. Guiding me into what was right and guiding me to you."

Even though the ring was a little loose, it was elegant and beautiful, and she loved it because of how important it was to Franz and that he was willing to give it to her.

He slid his father's ring onto his finger and peered down at his hand. "I've let fear and bitterness hold me back for too long, and I know now they would want me to move on with my life into this new adventure with you by my side."

Franz clasped her hand, holding their rings side by side. He kissed her fingers, then he bowed his head and whispered something in German—something that sounded like a prayer.

When he finished, he looked up at her and smiled, his eyes filling with both joy and peace.

She caressed his cheek, letting that joy and peace filter into her. They indeed would have a new adventure ahead. Together. And that was all she needed.

Author's Note

Dear Reader,

Thank you for joining me on another adventure into the high country of Colorado! I hope you enjoyed getting to know sweet Clarabelle Oakley. You might be thinking that Clementine's story comes next. But you'll have to wait a little longer for Clementine's happily-ever-after because Ryder's story is up next.

Yes, Ryder's story was just calling out to be written! As a single dad with a newborn babe, his situation was pretty dire, and I had to help him out and give him a wife. So the next book in the series, *A Wife for the Rancher*, is a fun mail-order bride and marriage of convenience story. I hope you'll love getting to meet Ryder's bride, a wealthy heiress who is running and hiding from her family. Of course, as usual, the story has plenty of sizzling (but clean!) romance and lots of adventure.

As always, I love hearing from YOU! If you haven't

yet joined my Facebook Reader Room, what are you waiting for!? It's a great place to keep up to date on all my book releases and book news, as well as a fun place to connect with other readers and me.

Finally, the more reviews a book has, the more likely other readers are to find it. If you have a minute, please leave a rating or review. I appreciate all reviews, whether positive or negative.

Until next time . . .

If you enjoyed **Willing to Wed the Rancher**, then make sure to read **Waiting for the Rancher**, the first book in the High Country Ranch series!

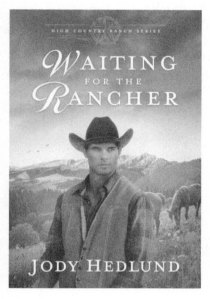

Hazel Noble loves her job managing the mares at High Country Ranch. As the foaling season begins, she gets to spend even more time with the horses . . . and with her secret crush, Maverick Oakley, the owner of High Country Ranch and her brother Sterling's best friend.

When Maverick unwittingly ruins Sterling's wedding, he goes from best friend to worst enemy. With the rift between their families, Maverick is faced with the possibility of losing Hazel, and he can no longer deny how much he's always cared about her. The trouble is that he and Sterling made a vow not to court each other's sisters, and he doesn't want to break his word and cause further problems.

Maverick gathers the courage to speak with Sterling about their vow, but Sterling demands that he stay away from

Hazel. When a tragic accident strikes, Maverick is forced to finally choose where his loyalties lie—with his best friend or his best friend's sister. After pushing Hazel away, will he be too late to win her heart?

- Charming flirt
- Best friend's sister
- Friends to more
- Secret crush
- Emotional scars
- Unexpected injury
- Horse ranch

"This one's worth rounding up."—Booklist, on *Falling for the Cowgirl*

*All of the books in the High Country Ranch series are sweet, closed-door romances with plenty of sizzle. The inspirational themes are light, and the romance is the main focus of the books.

Next up in the High Country Ranch series is…

A Wife for the Rancher

Millionaire heiress, Genevieve Hollis, has everything she wants except one thing, freedom, because her guardian stepmother insists on overseeing every move she makes. When Genevieve sees a newspaper advertisement from a rancher seeking a mother for his baby, she jumps at the chance to escape, even if that means hiding her true identity.

Ryder Oakley has suffered the repeated misfortune of losing the people he loves most, so now that he's a single father with a newborn baby, he's determined not to lose his son. When a woman shows up in answer to his advertisement, he quickly forms a marriage of convenience—one without all the entanglements of a real relationship.

When attraction starts to grow between the newly married couple, the secrets of their pasts threaten to catch up to them, and Ryder finds himself in a custody battle over his baby. As Genevieve struggles to outwit her stepmother, Ryder faces the threat of more losses. Will they be able to overcome the odds and find a way to be together before it's too late?

- Wealthy heiress
- Single dad
- Mail-order bride
- Marriage of convenience
- Hidden identity
- Forced proximity
- Opposites attract

The third book in the High Country Ranch series is not to be missed!

If you enjoyed *Willing to Wed the Rancher*, then check out more sweet Western romances by Jody Hedlund:

Committing to the Cowgirl

After years away, Astrid Nilsson has returned home to Colorado, hoping to become Fairplay's second doctor and to find healing for her reoccurring consumption. Dr. Logan Steele is seeking to hire a male physician to take over his clinic after he goes back East. When Astrid, his childhood sweetheart, insists that she's the one for the job, he offers her a bargain she can't refuse: pretend to court him to appease his mother and he'll give her the doctor position on a trial basis.

Cherishing the Cowgirl

Charity Courtney is at her wit's end trying to save her boardinghouse from a bank foreclosure. Wealthy railroad magnate Hudson Vanderwater hears of Charity's plight. Although he comes across as cold and callous, he is drawn to helping women in need because of a tragedy that destroyed his sister. He concocts a plan that will save Charity—he'll employ her and rent her boardinghouse for the month and in doing so alleviate her debt.

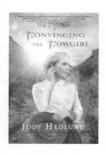

Convincing the Cowgirl

When unexpected visitors arrive at the Courtney Boardinghouse and claim the place belongs to them, Patience Courtney finds herself homeless and penniless. When wealthy rancher, Spencer Wolcott, proposes a marriage of convenience, Patience accepts the arrangement. In exchange for a new home, she agrees to become the mother to Spencer's precocious little girl so that he can manage his prosperous ranch.

Captivated by the Cowgirl

Now that her sisters are both married, Felicity Courtney manages the Courtney Boardinghouse alone. After nearly collapsing from exhaustion while caring for an invalid man and his wife who are staying at the boardinghouse, Felicity posts an advertisement for a hired hand. Philip Berg, a prince in disguise, is hiding in Fairplay while attempting to stay one step ahead of an assassin. When the spirited Felicity Courtney tacks up a notice that she is hiring help, he offers to do the job.

Claiming the Cowgirl

Serena Taylor is hiding in Colorado's high country to keep her son safe, and she knows the best way to protect him is by marrying again and giving him a father. Weston Oakley needs a wife by Christmas to placate his meddling family, but after being spurned one too many times in love, he's reluctant to give his heart away again. When they agree on a marriage of convenience, both of them get much more than they bargained for.

Jody Hedlund is the bestselling author of more than fifty novels and is the winner of numerous awards. Jody lives in Michigan with her husband, busy family, and five spoiled cats. She writes sweet historical romances with plenty of sizzle.

A complete list of my novels can be found at jodyhedlund.com.

Would you like to know when my next book is available? You can sign up for my newsletter, become my friend on Goodreads, like me on Facebook, or follow me on Instagram.

Newsletter: jodyhedlund.com

Facebook: AuthorJodyHedlund

Instagram: @JodyHedlund

Made in the USA
Middletown, DE
03 October 2024

61967903R00177